Wolff decid............ ....med himself with a beamer, a knife, a bow, and a quiverful of arrows. The weapons were primitive compared to the highly technological death-dispensers he would have to face.

He walked into the narrow space inside the hexaculum-entrance to Urizen's world. Wind whistled and tore at him. Blackness. A sense as of great hands gripping him. All in a dizzying flash.

He was standing upon grass, a blue sea close by, a red sky above. His clothes were still upon his body, and his weapons were still with him. He turned to see the hexaculum which had received him. It was not there.

Urizen had set another gate within his hexaculum and had shunted him off to this place, wherever it was. Wolff knew what would happen if he tried to walk back through the gate. Nevertheless, he did attempt it.

It was a one-way gate, as he had expected.

Somebody coughed behind him, and he whirled, his beamer ready.

The World of Tiers Series:

THE MAKER OF UNIVERSES

THE GATES OF CREATION

A PRIVATE COSMOS—forthcoming

BEHIND THE WALLS OF TERRA—
   forthcoming

THE LAVALITE WORLD—forthcoming

Also by Philip José Farmer:

THE STONE GOD AWAKENS

THE WIND WHALES OF ISHMAEL

THE GATES OF CREATION

by
Philip José Farmer

ace books
A Division of Charter Communications Inc.
A GROSSET & DUNLAP COMPANY
360 Park Avenue South
New York, New York 10010

THE GATES OF CREATION

An ACE Book

I

THOUSANDS OF YEARS AGO, the Lords had used drugs, electronics, hypnotism, and psychotechniques to do without sleep. Their bodies stayed fresh and vigorous, their eyes unclouded, for days and nights, for months. But their minds eventually crumbled. Hallucinations, unbounded anger, and an unreasonable sense of doom gripped them. Some went mad forever and had to be killed or imprisoned.

It was then that the Lords found that even they, makers of universes, owners of a science that put them only one step below the gods, must dream. The unconscious mind, denied communication with the sleeping conscious, revolted. Its weapon was madness, with which it toppled the pillars of reason.

So, all Lords now slept and dreamed.

Robert Wolff, once called Jadawin, Lord of the Planet of Many Levels, of a world that was constructed like a Tower of Babylon, dreamed.

He dreamed that a six-pointed star had drifted through a window into his bedroom. Whirling, it hung in the air above the foot of his bed. It was a *pandoogaluz*, one of the ancient symbols of the religion in which the Lords no longer believed. Wolff, who tended to think mostly in English, thought of it as a hexaculum. It was a six-sided star, its center glowing white, each of its facets flashing a ray, a scarlet, an orange, an azure, a purple, a black, and a yellow. The hexaculum pulsed like the heart of the sun, and the rays javelined out, raking his eyelids lightly. The beams scratched the skin as a house cat might extend a claw to wake its sleeping master with the tiniest sting.

"What do you want?" Wolff said, and knew he was dreaming. The hexaculum was a danger; even the shadows that formed between its beams were thick with evil. And he knew that the hexaculum had been sent by his father, Urizen, whom he had not seen for two thousand years.

"Jadawin!"

The voice was silent, the words formed by the six rays, which now bent and coiled and writhed like snakes of fire. The letters into which they shaped themselves were of the ancient alphabet, the original writing of the Lords. He saw them glowing before him, yet he understood them not so much through the eye as through a voice that spoke deep within him. It was as if the colors reached into the center of his mind and evoked a long-dead voice. The voice was deep, so deep it vibrated his innermost being, whirled it, and threatened to bend it into nightmare figures that would forever keep their shape.

"Wake up, Jadawin!" his father's voice said. By these words, Wolff knew that the flashing-rayed hexaculum was not only in his mind but existed in reality. His eyes opened, and he stared up at the concave ceiling, self-luminous with a soft and shifting light, veined with red, black, yellow, and green. He put out his left hand to touch Chryseis, his wife, and found that her side of the bed was empty.

At this, he sat upright and looked to left and right and saw that she was not in the room. He called, "Chryseis!" Then he saw the glittering pulsing six-rayed object that hung six feet above the edge of his bed. Out of it came, in sound, not fire, his father's voice.

"Jadawin, my son, my enemy! Do not look for the lesser being you have honored by making your mate. She is gone and will not be back."

Wolff stood up and then sprang out of bed. How had this thing gotten into his supposedly impregnable castle? Long before it had reached the bedroom in the center of the castle, alarms should have wakened him, massive doors should have slid shut throughout the enormous building, laser beams should have been triggered in the many halls, ready to cut down intruders, the hundred different traps should have been set. The hexaculum should have been shattered, slashed, burned, exploded, crushed, drowned.

But not a single light shone on the great wall across the room, the wall that seemed only an arabesqued decoration but was the alarm and control diagrampanel of the castle. It glimmered quietly as if an uninvited guest were not within a million miles.

The voice of Urizen, his father, laughed, and said, "You did not think you could keep the Lord of Lords out with your puny weapons, did you? Jadawin, I could kill you now where you stand gaping so foolishly, so pale and quivering and filmed in sweat."

"Chryseis!" Wolff cried out again.

"Chryseis is gone. She is no longer safe in your bed and in your universe. She has been taken as quickly and as silently as a thief steals a jewel."

"What do you want, Father?" Wolff asked.

"I want you to come after her. Try to get her back."

Wolff bellowed, leaped up onto the bed, and launched himself over its edge at the hexaculum. For that moment, he forgot all reason and caution, which had told him that the object could be fatal. His hands gripped the many-colored glowing thing. They closed on air and came together and he was standing on the floor, looking up above him at the space where the hexaculum had been. Even as his hands touched the area filled by the starred polyhedron, it had vanished.

So, perhaps, it had not been physical. Perhaps it had after all been a projection stirred in him by some means.

He did not believe so. It was a configuration of energies, of fields momentarily held together and transmitted from some remote place. The projector might be in the universe next door or it might be a million universes away. The distance did not matter. What did matter was that Urizen had penetrated the walls of Wolff's personal world. And he had spirited Chryseis away.

Wolff did not expect any more word from his father. Urizen had not indicated where he had taken Chryseis, how Wolff was to find her, or what would be done to Chryseis. Yet Wolff knew what he had to do. Somehow, he would have to locate the hidden self-enclosed cosmos of his father. Then he would have to find the gate that would give entrance to the pocket universe. At the same time that he got access, he would have to detect and avoid the traps set for him by Urizen. If he succeeded in doing this—and the probabilities were very low—he would have to get to Urizen and kill him. Only thus could he rescue Chryseis.

This was the multimillennia-old pattern of the game played among the Lords. Wolff himself, as Jadawin, the seventh som of Urizen, had survived 10,000 years of the deadly amusement. But he had managed to do so largely by being content with staying in his own universe. Unlike many of the Lords, he had not grown tired of the world he had created. He had enjoyed it—although it had been a cruel enjoyment, he had to admit now. Not only had he exploited the natives of his world for his own purposes, he had set up defenses that had snared more than one Lord—male and female, some his own brothers and sisters—and the trapped ones had died slowly and horribly. Wolff felt contrition for what he had done to the inhabitants of his planet. For the Lords he had killed and tortured, he suffered no guilt. They knew what they were doing when they came into his world, and if they had beaten his defenses, they would have given him a painful time before he died.

Then Lord Vannax had succeeded in hurling him into the universe of Earth, although at the cost of being taken along with Jadawin. A third Lord, Arwoor, had moved in to possess Jadawin's world.

Jadawin's memory of his former life had been repressed by the shock of dispossession, of being cast weaponless into an alien universe and without the means to return to his own world; Jadawin had become a blank, a *tabula rasa*. Adopted by a Kentuckian named Wolff, the amnesiac Jadawin had taken the name of Robert Wolff. Not until he was sixty-years old did he discover what had happened before the time that he had stumbled down a Kentucky mountain. He had retired from a lifetime of teaching Latin, Greek, and Hebrew to the Phoenix area of Arizona. And there, while looking through a newly built house for sale, he had begun the series of adventures that took him through a "gate" back into the universe he had created and had ruled as Lord for 10,000 years.

There he had fought his way up from the lowest level of the monoplanet, an Earth-sized Tower of Babylon, to the palace-castle of Lord Arwoor. There he had met and fallen in love with Chryseis, one of his own semicreations. And he had become the Lord again, but not the same Lord as the one who had left it. He had become human.*

His tears, loosed by his anguish at the loss of Chryseis and the terror of what could happen to her, were proof of his humanity. No Lord shed tears over another living being, although it was said that Urizen had cried with joy when he had trapped two of his sons some thousands of years ago.

*Wolff's story is told in *The Maker of Universes*, Philip José Farmer, Ace.

No time-waster, Wolff set about doing what had to be done. First, he must make sure that someone occupied the castle while he was gone. He did not want to repeat what had happened the last time he had left this world. On returning, he had found another Lord in his place. Now there was only one man who was capable of filling his shoes and whom he could trust. That was Kickaha (born Paul Janus Finnegan in Terre Haute, Indiana, Earth). It was Kickaha who had given him the horn that had enabled him to get back into this world. Kickaha had given him the indispensable help that had permitted him to regain his Lordship.

The horn!

With that, he would be able to track down Urizen's world and gain entrance to it! He strode across the chrysoprase floor to the wall and swung down a section of the wall, carved in the semblance of a giant eagless of this planet. He stopped and gasped with shock. The hiding place no longer had a horn to hide. The hollowed out part in which the horn had lain was empty.

So, Urizen had not only taken Chryseis but he had stolen the ancient Horn of Shambarimen.

So be it. Wolff would weep over Chryseis but he would spend no time in useless mourning for an artifact, no matter how treasured.

He walked swiftly through the halls, noting that none of the alarms were triggered. All slept as if this were just another day in the quiet but happy times since Wolff had regained possession of the palace on top of the world. He could not help shivering. He had always feared his father. Now that he had such evidence of his father's vast powers, he dreaded him even more. But he did not fear to go after him. He would track him down and kill him or die trying.

In one of the colossal control rooms, he seated

himself before a pagoda-shaped console. He set a control which would automatically bring him, in sequence, views of all the places on this planet where he had set videos. There were ten thousand of these on each of the four lower levels, disguised as rocks or trees. They had been placed to allow him to see what was happening in various key areas. For two hours he sat while the screen flashed views. Then, knowing that he could be there for several days, he plugged in the eidolon of Kickaha and left the viewer. Now, if Kickaha were seen, the screen would lock on the scene and an alarm would notify Wolff.

He placed ten more consoles in operation. These automatically began to scan throughout the cosmos of the "parallel" universes to detect and identify them. The records were seventy years old, so it was to be presumed that universes created since then would swell the known number of one thousand and eight. It was these that Wolff was interested in. Urizen no longer lived in the original one of Gardazrintah, where Wolff had been raised with many of his brothers, sisters, and cousins. In fact, Urizen, who grew tired of entire worlds as swiftly as a spoiled child became weary with new toys, had moved three times since leaving Gardazrintah. And the chances were that he was now in a fourth and this last one had to be identified and penetrated.

Even when all had been recorded, he could not be sure that his father's universe was located. If a universe were entirely sealed off, it was undetectable. A universe could be found only through the "gates," each of which gave off a unique frequency. If Urizen wanted to make it really difficult for Wolff to find him, he could set up an on-off-on gate. This would open at regular intervals or at random times, depending upon Urizen's choice. And if it happened not to open at the time that Wolff's scanner was searching that "parallel corridor," it would not be detected. As far as the scanners were concerned, that area would be an "empty" one.

However, Urizen wanted him to come after him and so should not make it too difficult or impossible for him to do so.

Lords must eat. Wolff had a light breakfast served by a *talos*, one of the half-protein robots, looking like knights in armor, of which he had over a thousand. Then he shaved and showered in a room carved out of a single emerald. Afterwards, he clothed himself. He wore corduroy shoes, tight-fitting corduroy trousers, a corduroy short-sleeved shirt, open at the neck but with a collar that curved up in back, a broad belt of mammoth leather, and a golden chain around his neck. From the chain hung a red jade image of Shambarimen, given to him by the great artist and artificer of the Lords, when he, Wolff, had been a boy of ten. The red of the jade was the only bright color of his garments, the rest being a thrush-brown. When in the castle, he dressed simply or not at all. Only during the rare occasions when he went down to the lower levels for state ceremonies did he dress in the magnificent robes and complex hat of a Lord. In most of his descents, he went incognito, clad in the garments or nongarments of the local natives.

He left the walls of the castle to go out onto one of the hundreds of great balcony-gardens. There was an Eye sitting in a tree, a raven large as a bald eagle. He was one of the few survivors of the onslaught of the castle when Wolff had taken this world back from Arwoor. Now that Arwoor was dead, the ravens had transferred their loyalty to Wolff.

Wolff told the raven that he was to fly out and look for Kickaha. He would inform other Eyes of the Lord of his mission and also tell the eagles of Podarge. They must inform Kickaha that he was wanted at once. If Kickaha did get their message and came to the castle, only to find Wolff gone, he was to remain there as Lord *pro tem*. If, after a reasonable interval, Wolff did not return, Kickaha could then do whatever he wanted.

He knew that Kickaha would come after him and that it was no use forbidding him to do so.

The raven flew off, happy to have a mission. Wolff went back into the castle. The viewers were still searching, without success, for Kickaha. But the gate-finders, needing only microseconds to scan and identify, had gone through all the universes and were already on their sixth sweep. He allowed them to continue on the chance that some gates might be intermittent and the search scan and gate on-state had not coincided. The results of the first five searches were on paper, printed in the classical ideographs of the ancient language.

There were thirty-five new universes. Of these, only one had a single gate.

Wolff had the spectral image of this placed upon a screen. It was a six-pointed star with the center red instead of white as he had seen it. Red for danger.

As plainly as if Urizen had told him, he knew that this was the gate to Urizen's world. Here I am. Come and get me—if you dare.

He visualized his father's face, the handsome falcon features with large eyes like wet black diamonds. Lords were ageless, their bodies held in the physiological grip of the first twenty-five years of life. But emotions were stronger even than the science of the Lords—working with their ally, time, they slashed away at the rocks of flesh. And the last time he had seen his father, he had seen the lines of hate. God alone knew how deep they were now, since it was evident that Urizen had not ceased to hate.

As Jadawin, Wolff had returned his father's enmity. But he had not been like so many of his brothers and sisters in trying to kill him. Wolff had just not wanted to have anything at all to do with him. Now, he loathed him because of what he had done to innocent Chryseis. Now, he meant to slay him.

The fabrication of a gate which would match the frequency-image of the hexaculum-entrance to Urizen's world was automatic. Even so, it took twenty-two hours for the machines to finish the device. By then, the planetary viewers had all reported in. Kickaha was not in their line of sight. This did not mean that the elusive fellow was not on the planet. He could be just outside the scope of the viewers or he could be a hundred thousand places elsewhere. The planet had even more land area than Earth, and the viewers covered only a tiny part of it. Thus, it might be a long long time before Kickaha was apprehended.

Wolff decided not to waste any time. The second the matching hexaculum was finished, he went into action. He ate a light meal and drank water, since he did not know how long he might have to do without either once he stepped through the gate. He armed himself with a beamer, a knife, a bow, and a quiverful of arrows. The primitive weapons might seem curious arms to take along in view of the highly technological death-dispensers he would have to face. But it was one of the ironies of the Lords' technology that the set-ups in which they operated sometimes permitted such weapons to be effective.

Actually, he did not expect to be able to use any of his arms. He knew too well the many types of traps the Lords had used.

"And now," Wolff said, "it must be done. There is no use waiting any longer."

He walked into the narrow space inside the matching hexaculum.

Wind whistled and tore at him. Blackness. A sense as of great hands gripping him. All in a dizzying flash.

He was standing upon grass, giant fronds at a distance from him, a blue sea close by, a red sky above, hugging the island and the rim of the sea. There was light from every quarter of the heavens and no sun. His clothes were still upon his body, although he had felt as if they were being ripped off when he had gone through the gate. Moreover, his weapons were still with him.

Certainly, this was not the interior of Urizen's stronghold. Or, if it were, it was the most unconventional dwelling-place of a Lord that he had ever seen.

He turned to see the hexaculum which had received him. It was not there. Instead, a tall wide hexagon of purplish metal rose from a broad flat boulder. He remembered now that something had pushed him out through it and that he had had to take several steps to keep from falling. The energy that had shoved him had caused him to pass out of it and a few paces from the boulder.

Urizen had set another gate within his hexaculum and had shunted him off to this place, wherever it was. Why Urizen had done so would become apparent quickly enough.

Wolff knew what would happen if he tried to walk back through the gate. Nevertheless, not being one to take things for granted, he did attempt it. With ease, he stepped out on the other side upon the boulder.

It was a one-way gate, just as he had expected.

Somebody coughed behind him, and he whirled, his beamer ready.

II

THE LAND ENDED abruptly against the sea with no
intervening beach. The animal had just emerged from
the sea and was only a few feet from him. It squatted
like a toad on huge webbed feet, its columnar legs
folded as if they were boneless. The torso was
humanoid and sheathed in fat, with a belly that pro-
truded like that of a Thanksgiving goose. The neck
was long and supple. At its end was a human head,
but the nose was flat and had long narrow nostrils.
Tendrils of red flesh sprouted out around the mouth.
The eyes were very large and moss-green. There
were no ears. The pate was covered, like the face and
body, with a dark-blue oily fur.

"Jadawin!" the creature said. It spoke in the ancient language of the Lords. "Jadawin! Don't kill me!
Don't you know me?"

Wolff was shocked but not so much that he forgot
to look behind him. This creature could be trying to
distract him.

"Jadawin! Don't you recognize your own brother!"

Wolff did not know him. The frog-seal body, lack
of ears, blue fur, and squashed long-slitted nose
made identification too difficult. And there was
Time. If he had really called this thing brother, it
must have been millennia ago.

That voice. It dug away at the layers of dusty
memory, like a dog after an old bone. It scraped away
level after level, it . . .

He shook his head and glanced behind him and at
the feathery vegetation. "Who are you?" he asked.

The creature whined, and by this he knew that his
brother—if it were his brother—must have been imprisoned in that body for a long long time. No Lord
whined.

"Are you going to deny me? Are you like the others? They'd have nothing to do with me. They mocked at me, they spat upon me, they drove me away with kicks and laughs. They said . . ."

It clapped its flippers together and twisted its face and large tears ran from the moss-green eyes and down the blue cheeks. "Oh, Jadawin, don't be like the rest! You were always my favorite, my beloved! Don't be cruel like them!"

The others, Wolff thought. There had been others. How long ago?

Impatiently, he said, "Let's not play games—whoever you are. Your name!"

The creature rose on its boneless legs, muscles raising the fat that coated them, and took a step forward. Wolff did not back away, but he held the beamer steady. "That's far enough. Your name."

The creature stopped, but its tears kept on flowing. "You are as bad as the others. You think of nobody but yourself; you don't care what's happened to me. Doesn't my suffering and loneliness and agonies all this time—oh, this immeasureable time—touch you at all?"

"It might if I knew who you were," Wolff said. "And what's happened to you."

"Oh, Lord of the Lords! My own brother!"

It advanced another giant splayfoot, the wetness squishing from out under the webs. It held out a flipper as if beseeching a tender hand. Then it stopped, and the eyes flicked at a spot just to one side of Wolff. He jumped to his left and whirled, the beamer pointing to cover both the creature and whoever might have been behind him. There was no one.

And, as the thing had planned, it leaped for Wolff at the same time that Wolff jumped and turned. Its legs uncoiled like a catapult released and shot him forward. If Wolff had only turned, he would have been knocked down. Standing to one side, he escaped all but the tip of the thing's right flipper. Even that, striking his left shoulder and arm, was enough to send him staggering numbly to one side, making him drop the beamer. Wolff was enormously solid and powerful himself, with muscles and nerve impulses raised to twice their natural strength and speed by the Lords' science. If he had been a normal Earthman, he would have been crippled forever in his arm, and he would not have been able to escape the second leap of the creature.

Squalling with fury and disappointment, it landed on the spot where Wolff had been, sank on its legs as it they were springs, spun, and launched itself at Wolff again. All this was done with such swiftness that the creature looked as if it were an actor in a speeded-up film.

Wolff had succeeded in regaining his balance. He jumped out for the beamer. The shadow of the creature passed over him; its shrieking was so loud it seemed as if its lips were pressed against his ear. Then he had the beamer in his hands, had rolled over and over, and was up on his feet. By then the thing had propelled itself again towards him. Wolff reversed the beamer, and using his right hand, brought the light but practically indestructible metal stock down on top of the creature's head. The impact of the huge body hurled him backward; he rolled away. The sea-thing was lying motionless on its face, blood welling from its seal-like scalp.

Hands clapped, and he turned to see two human beings thirty yards away inland, under the shadow of a frond. They were male and female, dressed in the magnificent clothes of Lords. They walked towards him, their hands empty of weapons. Their only arms were swords in crude leather, or fish-skin, scabbards. Despite this seeming powerlessness, Wolff did not relax his guard. When they had approached within twenty yards of him, he told them to stop. The creature groaned and moved its head but made no effort to sit up. Wolff moved away from it to be outside its range of leap.

"Jadawin!" the woman called. She had a lovely contralto voice which stirred his heart and his memory. Although he had not seen her in five hundred or more years, he knew her then.

"Vala!" he said. "What are you doing here?" The question was rhetorical; he knew she must have also been trapped by their father. And now he recognized the man. He was Rintrah, one of his brothers. Vala, his sister, and Rintrah, his brother, had fallen into the same snare.

Vala smiled at him, and his heart sprang again. She was of all women he had known the most beautiful, with two exceptions. His lovely Chryseis and his other sister, Anana the Bright, surpassed her. But he had never loved Anana as he had Vala. Just as he had never hated Anana as he had Vala.

Vala applauded again, and said, "Well done, Jadawin! You have lost none of your skill or wits. That thing is dangerous, even if detestable. It cringes and whines and tries to gain your trust, and then, bang! It's at your throat! It almost killed Rintrah when he first came here and would have if I had not struck it unconscious with a rock. So, you see, I, too, have dealt with it."

"And why did you not kill it then?" Wolff said.

Rintrah smiled and said, "Don't you know your own little brother, Jadawin? That creature is your beloved, your cute little Theotormon."

Wolff said, "God! Theotormon! Who did this to him?"

Neither of the two answered, nor was an answer needed. This was Urizen's world; only he could have refashioned their brother thus.

Theotormon groaned and sat up. One flipper placed over the bloody spot on his head, he rocked back and forth and moaned. His lichen-green eyes glared at Wolff, and he silently mouthed vituperation he did not dare voice.

Wolff said, "You're not trying to tell me you spared his life because of fraternal sentiment? I know you better than that."

Vala laughed and said, "Of course not! I thought he could be used later on. He knows this little planet well, since he has been here such a long long time. He is a coward, brother Jadawin. He did not have the courage to test his life in the maze of Urizen; he stayed upon this island and became as one of the degenerate natives. Our father tired of waiting for him to summon up a nonexistent manhood. To punish him for his lack of bravery, he caught him and took him off to his stronghold, Appirmatzum. There he reshaped him, made him into this disgusting sea-thing. Even then, Theotormon did not dare to go through the gates into Urizen's palace. He stayed here and lived as a hermit, hating and despising himself, hating all other living beings, especially Lords.

"He lives upon the fruit of the islands, the birds and fish and other sea-things he can catch. He eats them raw, and he kills the natives and eats them when he gets a chance. Not that they don't deserve their fate. They are the sons and daughters of other Lords who, like Theotormon, were craven. They lived out their miserable lives upon this planet, had babies, raised these, and then died.

"Urizen did to them as he did to Theotormon. He took them to Appirmatzum, made them into loathsome shapes, and brought them back here. Our father thought that surely the monstering of them would make them hate him so much they would then test the trapdoor planets, try to get into Appirmat-zum, and revenge themselves. But they were cow-ards all. They preferred to live on, even in their stomach-turning metamorphosis, rather than die as true Lords."

Wolff said, "I have much to learn about this little arrangement of our father. But how do I know that I can trust you?"

Again Vala laughed. "All of us who have fallen into Urizen's traps are upon this island. Most of us have been here only a few weeks, although Luvah has been here for half a year."

"Who are the others?"

"Some of your brothers and cousins. Besides Rin-trah and Luvah, there are two other brothers, Enion and Ariston. And your cousins Tharmas and Palamabron."

She laughed merrily and pointed at the red sky and said, "All, all snared by our father! All gathered together again after a heartrending absence of mil-lennia. A happy family reunion such as mortals could not imagine."

"I can imagine," Wolff said. "You still have not answered my question about trust."

"We have all sworn to a common-front truce," Rintrah said. "We need each other, so we must put aside our natural enmity and work together. Only thus will it be possible to defeat Urizen."

"There hasn't been a common-front truce for as long as I can remember," Wolff said. "I remember Mother telling me that there had been one once, four thousand years before I was born, when the Black Bellers threatened the Lords. Urizen has performed two miracles. He has trapped eight Lords all at once, and he has forced a truce. May this be his downfall."

Wolff then said that he would swear to the truce. By the name of the Father of all Lords, the great

Eponym Los, he swore to observe all the rules of the peace-agreement until such time as all agreed to abandon it or all were dead but one. He knew even as he took the oath that the others could not be relied upon not to betray him. He knew that Rintrah and Vala were aware of this and trusted him no more than he did them. But at least they would all be working together for a while. And it was not likely that any would lightly break truce. Only when a great opportunity and strong likelihood of escaping punishment coincided would any do so.

Theotormon whined, "Jadawin. My own brother. My favorite brother, he who said he would always love me and protect me. You are like the others. You want to hurt me, to kill me. Your own little brother."

Vala spat at him and said, "You filthy craven beast! You are no Lord nor brother of ours. Why do you not dive to the deeps and there drown yourself, take your fearfulness and treachery out of our sight and the sight of all beings that breathe air? Let the fish feed upon your fat carcass, though even they may vomit you forth."

Crouching, extending a flipper, Theotormon shuffled towards Wolff. "Jadawin. You don't know how I've suffered. Is there no pity in you for me? I always thought you, at least, had what these others lacked. You had a warm heart, a compassion, that these soulless monsters lacked."

"You tried to kill me," Wolff said. "And you would try again if you thought you had a good chance of doing it."

"No, no," Theotormon said, attempting to smile. "You misunderstood me entirely. I thought you would hate me because I loved even a base life more than I did a death as a Lord. I wanted to take your weapons away so you couldn't hurt me. Then I would have explained what had happened to me, how I came to be this way. You would have understood then. You would have pitied me and loved me as you did when you were a boy in the palace of our father and I was your infant brother. That is all I wanted to do, explain to you and be loved again, not hated. I meant you no harm. By the name of Los, I swear it."

"I will see you later," Wolff said. "Now, for the present, be gone."

Theotormon walked away spraddle-legged. When he had reached the edge of the island, he turned and shouted obscenities and abuse at Wolff. Wolff raised his beamer, although he meant only to scare Theotormon. The thing squawked and leaped like a giant frog out over the water, his rubbery legs and webbed toes trailing behind him. He went into the water and did not come up again. Wolff asked Vala how long he could stay under the surface.

"I do not know. Perhaps half and hour. But I doubt that he is holding his breath. He is probably in one of the caverns that exist in the roots and bladders that form the base of this island."

She said that they must go to meet the others. While they walked through the frond-forest, she explained the physical facts of this world, as far as she knew them.

"You must have noticed how close the horizon is. This planet has a diameter of about 2170 miles." (About the size of earth's moon, Wolff thought.) "Yet the gravity is only a little less than that of our home-planet." (Not much stronger than Earth's, Wolff thought.)

"The gravity fades off abruptly above the atmosphere," she said, "and extends weakly through this universe. All the other planets have similar fields."

Wolff did not wonder at this. The Lords could do things with fields and gravitons that the terrestrials had never dreamed of as yet.

"This planet is entirely covered with water."

"What about this island?" he said.

"It floats. Its origin is a plant which grows on the bottom of the sea. When it's half-grown, it's bladder starts to fill with gas, produced by a bacteria. It unroots itself and floats to the surface. There it extends roots or filaments, which meet with the filaments of others of its kind. Eventually, there's a solid mass of such plants. The upper part of the plant dies off, while the lower part continues to grow. The decaying upper forms a soil. Birds add their excrement to it. They come to new islands from old islands, and bring seeds in their droppings. These produce the fronds you see and the other vegetation." She pointed at a clump of bamboo-like plants.

He asked, "Where did those rocks come from?"

There were several whitish boulders, with a diameter of about twelve feet, beyond the bamboos.

"The gas bladder plants that form islands are only one of perhaps several thousand species. There's a type that attaches itself to sea-bottom rocks and that carries the rock to the surface when they're buoyant enough. The natives bring them in and place them on the islands if they're not too big. The white ones attract the *garzhoo* bird for some reason, and the natives kill the *garzhoo* or domesticate it."

"What about the drinking water?"

"It's a fresh-water ocean."

Wolff, glancing through a break in the wilderness of purplish, yellow-streaked fronds and waist-high berry-burdened bushes, saw a tremendous black arc appear on the horizon. In sixty seconds, it had become a sphere and was climbing above the horizon.

"Our moon," she said. "Here, things are reversed. There is no sun; the light comes from the sky. So the moon provides night or absence of light. It is a pale sort of night, but better than none.

"Later, you will see the planet of Appirmatzum. It is in the center of this universe, and around it the five secondary planets revolve. You will see them, too, all black and sky-filling like our moon."

Wolff asked how she knew so much about the structure of Urizen's world. She answered that Theotormon had given the information, though not willingly. He had learned much while a prisoner of Urizen. He had not wanted to part with the information, since he was a surly and selfish beast. But when his brothers, cousins, and sister had caught him, they had forced him to talk.

"Most of the scars are healed up," she said. She laughed.

Wolff wondered if Theotormon did not have good reasons after all for wanting to kill them. And he wondered how much of her story of their dealings with him was true. He would have to have a talk with Theotormon some time, at a safe distance from him, of course.

Vala stopped talking and seized Wolff's arm. He started to jerk away, thinking that she meant to try some trick. But she was looking upwards with alarm and so was Rintrah.

THE FRONDS, sixty feet high, had hidden the object in the sky. Now he saw a mass at least a quarter-mile wide, fifty feet thick, and almost a mile long floating fifty feet in the air. It was drifting with the wind, which came from an unknown quarter of the compass. In this world without sun, north, south, east, and west meant nothing.

"What is that?" he said.

"An island that floats in the air. Hurry. We have to get to the village before the attack starts."

Wolff set off after the others. From time to time, he looked up through the fronds at the *aeronesus*. It was descending rather swiftly at the opposite end of the island. He caught up with Vala and asked her how the floater could be navigated. She replied that its inhabitants used valves in the giant bladders to release their hydrogen. This procedure required almost all the natives, since each bladder-valve was operated by hand. During a descent, they would all be occupied with the navigation.

"How do they steer it?"

"The bladders have vents. When the *abutal* want the island to go in one direction, they release gas from banks of bladders on the side opposite to that in which they want to go. They don't get much power thrust, but they're very skillful. Even so, they have to contend with the winds and don't always maneuver effectively. We've been attacked twice before by the *abutal*, and both times they missed our island. They'll drop sea-anchors—big stones on the ends of cables—to slow them down. The first attackers settled down close to our island instead of just above it and had to content themselves with an attack by sea. They failed."

She stopped, then said, "Oh, no! These must be the Ilmawir. Los help us."

At first, Wolff thought that the fifty craft that had launched from the floater were small airplanes. Then, as they circled to land against the wind, he saw that they were gliders. The wings, fifty feet long, were of some pale shimmering stuff and scalloped on the edges. A painted image of an eye with crossed swords above it was on the underside of each wing. The fuselage was an uncovered framework, and its structure and the rudder and ailerons were painted scarlet. The pilot sat in a wickerwork basket just forward of the monowings. The nose of the craft was rounded and had a long horn projecting to a length of about twenty feet in front of it. Like the horn of a narwhal, Wolff thought. As he later found out, the horns were taken from a giant fish.

A glider passed above them on a path which would make it land ahead of them. Wolff got a glimpse of the pilot. His red hair stood at least a foot high; the hair shone with some fixative oil. His face was painted like a red Indian's with red and green circles, and black chevrons ran down his neck and across his shoulders.

"The village is about a half-mile from here," Vala said. "On the extreme end of the island."

Wolff wondered why she was so concerned. What did a Lord care what happened to others? She explained that if the Ilmawir made a successful landing, they would kill every human being on the island. They would then plant some of their surplus people as a colony.

The island was not entirely flat. There were rises here and there, formed by the uneven growth of the bladders. Wolff climbed to the top of one and looked over the fronds. The *abuta* was down to fifty feet now, settling slowly and headed directly for the village. This was a group of about one hundred beehive-shaped huts, built of fronds. A wall twenty feet high surrounded the village. It looked as if it were constructed of stones, bamboo, fronds, and some dull gray poles that could be the bones of colossal sea-creatures.

Men and women were stationed behind the walls and several groups were out in the open. They were armed with spears and bows and arrows.

Beyond the village were docks built of bamboo. Along them and on the shore were boats of various builds and sizes. Its bottom was a dense tangle of thick roots. There were, however, openings in it, and from several of these large stones at the ends of cables of vegetable matter were dropped. The stones were white, gypsum-like, and carved into flat discs. They trailed in the sea as they were dragged along by the island, then struck the land. The cables of some caught under the docks.

Other anchors fell and struck against the walls of the village. They were snagged in the tangle of stuff forming the high-piled walls. They bumped along the grassless ground and slammed into the sides of the huts. These collapsed under the impact of the stones. At the same time, arrows were shot, spears and rocks dropped, and flaming objects cast from the hatches onto the people below. Some islanders were struck down; huts started to burn. The flaming objects exploded, and a dense black smoke rose from them.

The defenders, however, were not helpless. From a large central building came men and women with curious devices. They lit and released them, and they rose swiftly towards the underpart of the floater. They caught in the tangle of roots and burned there. Then they exploded, and fire spread among the roots.

The roof of a hut lifted up and fell over to one side, like the roof of a trapdoor spider. The walls collapsed in orderly fashion outwards, falling to the ground and forming a petal-figure. In the center of the hut was a catapult, a giant bow with an arrow made from the horns of the creature that had provided the booms on the noses of the gliders. To it were attached a number of flaming bladders. The bow was released, and the burning arrow shot upwards and buried itself deep within the under part of the floater.

The catapult crew began to wind the string back. A man fell from an opening in the floater and was followed by ten more. They came down as if parachuting. Their descent was checked by a cluster of bladders attached to a harness around the shoulders and chest. An arrow caught the first *abutal* just before he struck the ground, and then three more of the ten behind him were transfixed.

The survivors landed untouched a few feet from the catapult. They unstrapped their harness, and the bladders rose away from them. By then, they were surrounded. They fought so fiercely—one got to the catapult, only to be run through with two spears.

The island-floater, driven by the wind, began to pass over the village. Other stones on cables had been dropped, and a few had caught in the tangle of the walls without breaking. Then ropes fell onto the fronds and the huge loops tightened around them.

Caught at the forward end, the floater swung around so that its bulk hung over this part of the surface island. By then, the gliders had made their landing, not all successfully. Because of the density of the vegetation, the crafts had to come down upon fronds. Some were flipped over; some crashed through several fronds before being caught and held. Some slipped down between the fronds and smashed into the tough thick bushes.

But from where he stood, Wolff could see at least twenty pilots, unhurt, who were now slipping through the jungle. And there had to be others.

He heard his name called. Vala had come back and was standing at the foot of the hill.

"What do you intend to do?" she said angrily. "You have to take sides, Jadawin, whether you want to or not. The *abutal* will kill you."

"You may be right," he said as he came down the hill. "I wanted to get some idea of what was going on. I didn't want to rush blindly into this without knowing where everybody was, how the fight was going on. . . ."

"Always the cautious and crafty Jadawin," she said. "Well, that's all right; it shows you are no fool, which I already know. Believe me, you need me as much as I need you. You can't go this thing alone."

He followed her, and presently they came upon Rintrah, crouching under a frond. He gestured at them for silence. When they were beside him, Wolff looked at where Rintrah was pointing. Five *abutal* warriors were standing not twenty yards from them. The tail of a wrecked glider rose from behind a crushed bush to their left. They carried small round shields of bone, javelins of bone tipped with bamboo, and several had bows and arrows. The bows were made of some hornlike substance, were short and recurved, and formed of two parts that were joined in a central socket of horn. The warriors were too far away for him to overhear their conference.

"What's the range of your beamer?" Vala said.

"It kills up to fifty feet," he said. "Third-degree burns for the next twenty feet, and after that, second-degree burns up through a light singe to no effect."

"Now's your chance. Rush them. You can kill all five with one sweep before they know what's going on."

Wolff sighed. There would have been a time when

he would not even have waited for Vala's urgings. He would have killed them all by now and been tempted to continue the work with Vala and Rintrah. But he was no longer Jadawin; he was Robert Wolff. Vala would not understand this, or if she did, she would see his hesitation as a weakness. He did not want to kill, but he doubted that there was any way of forcing the *abutal* to call off their attack. Vala knew these people, and she was probably telling him the truth about them. So, like it or not, he had to take sides.

There was a yell behind them. Wolff rolled over and sat up to see three more *abutal* warriors about forty feet from them. They had burst out from behind a frond and were charging towards them, their javelins raised.

Wolff twisted around to face the three *abutal*, and he pressed on a plate on the underside of the three-foot long barrel. A dazzling white ray, pencil-thick, traced across the bellies of all three. The vegetation between and in back of them smoked. The three fell forward, the javelins dropping from their hands, and they slid on the grass, face down.

Wolff rose to one knee, turned, and faced the five. The two archers stopped and took aim. Wolff dropped them first, then the other three. He continued to crouch and looked about him for others who might have been attracted by the cries. Only the wind through the fronds and the hushed cries and muffled explosions of the battle at the village could be heard.

The odor of burned flesh sickened him. He rose and turned over the three corpses, then the five. He did not think that any were still alive, but he wanted to make sure. Each was almost cut in half by the beam. The skin along the gashes was crisped under the blood. There was not much blood, since the energy of the beam, absorbed by the bodies, had cooked their lungs and intestines. Their bowels, contracting, had ejected their contents.

Vala looked at the beamer. She was very curious but knew better than to ask Wolff if she could handle it. "You have two settings," she said. "What can it do on full power?"

"It can cut through a ten-foot slab of steel," he replied. "But the charge won't last more than sixty seconds. On half-power, it can project for ten minutes before needing recharging."

She looked at his pockets, and he smiled. He had no intention of telling her many fresh charges were in his pockets.

"What happened to your weapons?" he said.

Vala cursed and said, "They were stolen while we slept. I don't know whether Urizen or that slimy Theotormon did it."

He started to walk towards the battle; the two followed close behind. The island above threw them into a pale shadow which would be deepened soon when the night-bringing moon covered this side of the planet. Ilmawir, men and women both, were still dropping out of the openings in the bottom. Others, buoyed up by larger clusters of bladders, were working on the bottom as fire-fighters. They used many-faceted objects that, when squeezed, spurted out water.

"Those are living sea-creatures," she said. "Amphibians. They travel on land by spurting out jets of water and rolling with the thrusts."

Wolff set the beamer at full power. Whenever they came near a rope tangled in a tree or a stone anchor, he cut the cable loose. Three times he came across *abutal* and set the beamer on half-power. By the time he was a few yards from the village, he had severed forty cables and killed twenty-two men and women.

"A lucky thing for us you came when you did," Vala said. "I don't think we could have driven them off if you hadn't arrived."

Wolff shrugged. He ejected a power-pack and slipped another of the little cylinders into the breach. He had six left, and if this continued he would soon be out. But there was nothing he could do to conserve them.

The village was surrounded on the land side by about ninety *abutal*. Apparently, those who had dropped into the village had been wiped out, but the villagers were busy putting out fires. However, they no longer had to worry about attack from directly overhead. The Ilmawir island had been affected by the cutting of so many cables. It had slipped on downwind by a quarter-mile and only because a hundred other ropes and anchors had been used had it managed to keep from losing the surface-island altogether.

Wolff beamed the group of officers who were standing on top of the only hill near the village. Presently, the other *abutal* became aware of what was happening. Half left the siege to surround the hill. The area bristled with spears and arrows. The Lords would have been open to a concentrated fire of arrows, but they were protected behind a group of four white stone idols on the hill.

Vala said, "They're on the defensive now. If they don't know it now, they soon will. And that will be good for us. Perhaps . . ."

She was silent for a while. Wolff shot three men as they ran towards a hollow in the hill. He said, "Perhaps what?"

"Our beloved father left a message for us on this island. He told us some of what we have to do if we hope to get within his castle. Apparently, we have to find the gates which lead to him. There are none on this island. He says there is a pair on another island, but he did not say just where. We have to find them by ourselves, so I was thinking . . ."

A roar arose from the *abutals*, and the front lines rushed the hill. The archers sent a covering fire of at least thirty arrows per volley. Vala and Rintrah cowered behind an idol, as Wolff had told them to do. Much as he hated to expend his power, he was forced to do so. He put the beamer on full and shot over the heads of the front lines. Smoke arose from vegetation and flesh alike as he described a circle with the white ray. The archers had had to expose themselves to get good shots, and so most fell.

Arrows rattled around Wolff, leaping off the stone idols. One creased his shoulder; another ricocheted off stone and flew between his legs. Then, there were no more arrows. The *abutal* in the second ranks, seeing those crumple before them, smelling the fried flesh, wavered. Wolff began on them, and they fled back into the jungle.

"You were thinking?" he said to Vala.

"We could search a thousand years, using this island as our ship, and not find one island that has the gates. Perhaps that is Father's idea. He would enjoy seeing us in a futile search, enjoy our despair. And the friction and murder that such long association would make inevitable among us. But if we were on an *abuta*, which would enable us not only to travel faster but to see far more from its altitude . . ."

"It's a fine idea," he said. "How do we talk the *abutal* into letting us accompany them? And what guarantee is there that they would not turn on us the first chance they got?"

"You have forgotten much about your younger sister. How could you, of all who have loved me, not remember how persuasive I can be?"

She stood up and shouted at the seemingly unin-

habited jungle. For a while there was no response.
She repeated her demands. Presently, an officer
walked out from behind a frond. He was a tall well-
built man in his early thirties, handsome behind the
garish circles on his face. Besides the black chevrons
down neck and shoulders, he was decorated with a
painted seabird on his chest. This was an *iiphtarz*,
and it indicated a commander of the glider force.
Behind him came his wife, clad in a short skirt of red
and blue seabird feathers, her red hair coiled on top
of her head, her face painted with green and white
lozenges, a necklace of fingerbones around her neck,
an *iiphtarz* painted across her breasts, and three concentric circles of crimson, black, and yellow painted
around her navel. As was the custom among the
abutal, she accompanied her husband in battle. If he
died, it was her duty to attack his killers until she
slew them or died herself.

The two advanced up the hill until Wolff told them
to come no further. Vala began talking, and the man
began to smile. His wife, however, watched Vala
closely and scowled throughout the conversation.

IV

DUGARNN, THE OFFICER, capitulated only when certain terms had been agreed upon. He refused to leave the island until he had gotten at least part of what the Ilmawir had intended to take when they attacked. Vala did not hesitate to promise him that the defenders' domestic fowl and animals (sea-rats and small seals) would be his prize of war. Moreover, the *abutal* could mutilate the corpses of their enemies and scalp them.

The surface-islanders, who called themselves Friiqan, objected when they heard these terms. Wolff told their leaders that if they did not accept, they would find the war continued. And he, Wolff, would take no sides this time. Surlily, they said they would do as he wished. The *abutal* stripped the villagers of everything they considered valuable.

The other Lords—Luvah, Enion, Ariston, Tharmas, and Palamabron—had been in the village when the attack started. They were very surprised to see him, and they could not hide their envy of his beamer. Only Luvah seemed glad to see him. Luvah, the runt of the lot, was sandy-haired and fine-featured except for a broad and full mouth. His eyes were a deep blue, and he had a faint milky way of freckles across the bridge of his nose and cheeks. He threw his arms around Wolff and hugged him and even wept a little. Wolff permitted the embrace because he did not believe that Luvah would take the chance to stab him. As children, the two had always been close, and had much in common, both being imaginative and inclined to let others do and think as they wished. In fact, Luvah had never idulged in the Lords' deadly game of trying to dispossess or slay the others.

"How did our father manage to entice you out from your world, where you were safe and happy?" Wolff said.

Luvah grinned crookedly and said, "I might ask you the same thing. Perhaps he played the same trick on you as on me. He sent a messenger, a glowing hexaculum, and it said that it was sent by you. You wanted me to come visit you; you were lonely and wished to talk again to the one member of your family who did not want to kill you. So, after taking what I thought were good precautions, I left my universe. I entered what I thought was your gate, only to find myself on this island."

Wolff shook his head and said, "You were always too impetuous, brother, too rash. Yet, I feel honored that you would forsake your safety to visit me. Only . . ."

"Only I should have been much more careful, more sure that the messenger was from you. At another time, I might have been. But at the moment the hexaculum arrived, I was thinking of you and longing for you. Even we Lords have our weaknessess, you know."

Wolff was silent for a while, watching the exultant Ilmawir carry away fowl, animals, necklaces, and rings of sea-jade. Then he said, "We are in the most desperate situation we have ever faced, Luvah. The greatest peril, of course, is our father. But almost as deadly are those on whom we have to depend most. Despite their word of honor, they will always need watching. Now I propose that we support each other. When I sleep, you watch. When you sleep, I stand guard."

Luvah smiled one-sidedly again and said, "And when you sleep, you will keep one eye open to watch me, heh, brother?"

Wolff frowned, and Luvah said hastily, "Do not be

angry, Jadawin. You and I have managed to survive so long because we never fully gave our trust. With the best of reasons. How sad it is that all of us, our sisters, brothers, and cousins, once lived and studied and played together in innocence and even love. Yet, today, we are as hungry wolves at each others' throats. And why, I ask you? Why? I will tell you. It is because the Lords are mad. They think they are gods, when all the time they are only human beings, really no better than these savages here. Only they happen to be heir to a great power, a science and technology which they use without understanding the principles behind it. They are as evil children with toys that create whole worlds and destroy whole worlds. The great and wise men who devised the toys have long since died; knowledge and science have died out; and the good inherent in the cosmic powers is twisted for their benefit and theirs only."

"I know that well, brother," Wolff said. "Better than you, perhaps, since I was once as selfish and vicious as those others. Yet I underwent an experience which I will tell you about sometime. It changed me into a human being—I hope—into a being only you have the ability to appreciate."

The Ilmawir had dropped great balloon-like ladders with weights on them from the *abuta*. The loot was tied to these and floated back up along guide-ropes into the hatches in the bottom of the island. Those gliders worth repairing were also returned to the floater. When the stripping of the Friiqan was done, the *abutal* ascended. Wolff rode up in a harness attached to a pair of bladders. He held his beamer ready, since now the *abutal* had him in a position where they could attempt murder and have some hope of success. However, no moves were made. He rose through the opening and was seized by two grinning women. They dragged him to one side and unharnessed him. The bladders were taken into the dim interior of a large chamber, where other bladders were stored.

When all the Lords were landed, they were led by Dugarnn and his woman, Sythaz, up a winding flight of steps to the upper part of the island. The stairs were made of very light, paper-thin but strong material. This was the hardened shell of gas-bladders. On the *abuta*, where weight was critical, everything was as light as possible. This consideration had even affected the language as he was to discover. Although the speech differed little in basic vocabulary from the parent, it had undergone some sound changes. And new words relating to weight, shape, flexibility, size, and vertical and horizontal direction had arisen. These were used as classifiers in a sense unknown to the pristine speakers. Indeed, no noun and few adjectives could be used without accompanying classifiers. In addition, a detailed nautical and aeronavigational terminology had arisen.

The stairwell was a shaft cut through a hard tangle of roots. On coming out at its top, he found himself on the floor of a sort of amphitheater. The floor was made of broad strips of bladder-covering, and the sloping walls were composed of huge bladders tied together with roots. There was only one building on the great deck, a thatch-roofed opensided longhouse. This was the social and recreational building. It had flat stones on which each family cooked the meals. Domestic fowl and sea-rats ran loose, and meat-seals played in an inch-deep pool of water near the center.

Sythaz, the commander's wife, showed them where they would live. These quarters consisted of cubicles cut out of the roots and floored and walled with bladder-shells. Openings were cut in the floor and descent was made by a portable ladder. The only light came from through the hatch or from small fish-oil lamps. There was just enough room to take two steps one way and two another. The beds were coffin-shaped holes in the wall in which were mattresses of feathers stuffed into sealskin. Most of the daily and nightly activity took place on the "main-deck." There was absolutely no privacy except in the chief's bridge.

Wolff had expected the *abutal* to hoist anchor and sail off at once. Dugarnn said that they must wait a while. For one thing, the island needed more altitude before it could start out over the open seas. The bacteria that generated gas in the bladders worked very fast when fed nutrient, but it still would take two days before the bladders were filled enough for Dugarnn to consider it safe to cast loose.

Secondly, the invasion had cost the *abutal* a relatively staggering number of casualties. There were just not enough people to work the island efficiently. So, Dugarnn proposed something that the *abutal* had not had to do for a long time. The shortage of population would be made up by recruiting from the Friiqan. After making sure his "guests" knew where they were to be quartered, Dugarnn went back to the surface. Wolff, curious, accompanied him. Vala insisted on going with him. Whether this was to satisfy her curiosity or just to keep an eye on him, Wolff did not know. Probably, she had both motives.

Dugarnn explained to the chief of the Friiqan what he wanted. The chief, dispirited, waved a hand to indicate that he did not care what happened. Dugarnn gathered the survivors together and made his offer. To Wolff's surprise, many volunteered. Vala told him that the two peoples were thorough enemies, but that the Friiqan had lost face. Moreover, many of the young considered an aerial life as romantic.

Dugarnn looked the volunteers over and picked

out those who had distinguished themselves during the fighting. He chose more women than men, especially those with children. There was an initial ceremony of ritual torture, which consisted of lightly burning the candidate on his or her groin. Normally, a captured enemy was tortured to death unless he exhibited exceptional stoicism and bravery. Then he could be initiated into the tribe.

In emergencies, such as now, the torture was only token.

Later, after the island had set sail, the initiates would go through a ceremony in which each would mingle his blood with that of an Ilmawir. This prevented revenge from the surface-people, since blood-brotherhood was sacred.

"There's another reason besides needing more crew," Vala said. "The *abutal*—in fact both surface and air islanders—have a tendency to inbreed. To avoid this, prisoners are sometimes adopted into the tribe."

She was very friendly with Wolff now and insisted on being with him every moment. She had even resumed calling him *wivkrath*, the Lords' term for "darling." She leaned against him every time she had a chance and once even gave him a light kiss on the cheek. Wolff did not respond. He had not forgotten, even after 500 years, that they had been lovers and yet she had tried to kill him.

Wolff set out for the area of the gate through which he had entered. Vala went with him. To her questions, he answered that he wanted to talk to Theotormon once more.

"That sea-slug! What can he have that you would want?"

"Information, perhaps."

They came to the gate. Theotormon was not in sight. Wolff walked along the edge of the island, noting that here and there the land sank slightly under his weight. Apparently, the bladders were not so thick in these places.

"How many of these islands are there on this planet and what is the maximum size?" he said.

"I do not know. We have sighted two since we've been here, and the Friiqan say that there are many more. They speak of the Mother of Islands, a relatively huge island that they claim to have heard of. There are many aerial islands, too, but none larger than the Ilmawirs'. Why do you want to talk of boring things like that, when we have ourselves to discuss?"

"Like what?" he said.

She faced him, so close that her upraised lips almost touched his chin. "Why can't we forget what happened to us? After all, that was a long time ago, when we were much younger and therefore not so wise."

"I doubt that you've changed," he said.

She smiled and said, "How would you know? Let me prove that I am different now."

She put her arms around him and placed her head on his chest.

"Different in everything but one. I loved you once, and now that I see you again, I realize I've never really stopped loving you."

"Even when you tried to murder me in my bed?" he said.

"Oh, that! Darling, I thought you were with that loathsome and conniving Alagraada. I thought you were betraying me. Can you blame me because I crazed with jealousy? You know how terribly possessive I am."

"I know only too well." He pushed her away and said, "Even as a child, you were selfish. All Lords are selfish, but few to the degree to which you were. I cannot see now why I ever loved you."

"You toad!" she cried. "You loved me because I am Vala. That's all, just that I am Vala."

He shook his head and said, "That may have been true once. But it is not true any longer. Nor will it ever be true again."

"You love another! Do I know her? It's not Anana, not my stupid murderous sister."

"No," he said. "Anana is murderous, but she's not stupid. She didn't fall into Urizen's trap. I don't see her here. Or has something happened to her? Is she dead?"

Vala shrugged, turned away, and said, "I haven't heard of her for three hundred years. But your concern shows that you do care for her. Anana! Who would have thought it?"

Wolff did not try to change her mind. He did not think that it was wise to mention Chryseis, even though Vala might never have contact with her. There was no use taking a chance.

Vala spun around and said, "What happened to that Earth girl?"

"What Earth girl?" he said, taken aback at her viciousness.

"What Earth girl?" she mimicked. "I mean that Chryseis, the mortal you abducted from Earth some two and a half millennia ago. From a region the Earthlings call Troy or something like that. You made her immortal, and she became your mistress."

"Along with quite a few thousand others," he said. "Why pick on her?"

"Oh, I know, I know. You have really become degenerate, my brother Wolff-Jadawin."

"So you know my Earth name, the name by which I prefer to be called? And how much else do you know about me? And why?"

"I've always made it my business to have as much

information about the Lords as it is possible to get," she said. "That is why I have stayed alive so long."

"And why so many others have died."

Her voice became soft again, and she smiled at him. "There's no reason for you to pick a quarrel with me. Why can't we let bygones be bygones?"

"Who picked a quarrel? No, there's no reason why bygones can't be just that, provided they are bygones. But the Lords never remember a good turn or forget an injury. And until you've convinced me otherwise, I will regard you as the same old Vala. As beautiful, maybe even more beautiful, but still with a black and rotten soul."

She tried to smile. "You always were too blunt. Maybe that was one reason why I loved you so much. And you were more of a man than the others. You were the greatest of all my lovers."

She waited for him to return the compliment. Instead, he said, "Love is what makes a lover. I did love you. *Did*."

He walked away from her along the edge of the shore. He looked back from time to time. She was following him at a distance of twenty feet. Now and then, the earth sank beneath his feet. He stopped for her to catch up with him and said, "There must be many caves on the bottom. How can Theotormon be called out?"

"He can't. There are many caves, yes. Sometimes a whole group of bladders die, either from disease, old age, or from being eaten by a fish which finds them tasty. Then caverns exist for a while, although they're eventually filled up by new growths."

Wolff filed this information away for possible use. If things went too badly, a man could always take refuge under the island. Vala must have guessed what he was thinking—a gift he had found irritating when they had been mates—and she said, "I wouldn't go under there. The water swarms with man-eaters.''

"How does Theotormon survive?''

"I don't know. Maybe he's too fast and strong for the fish. After all, he's adapted for that kind of life—if you want to call it a life.''

Wolff decided that he would have to give up on Theotormon. He walked back into the jungle with Vala close behind. By now he permitted her to be at his back. She needed him too much to kill him.

He had gone only a few yards when he was knocked down from behind. At first, he thought that she had leaped upon him. He rolled away from her, trying to draw his beamer from its holster at the same time. He saw then that she had been propelled into him by another. The huge glistening wet body of Theotormon was flying at him. The bulk came flat down on him, and his breath was knocked out by the impact of 400 pounds. Then Theotormon was sitting on top of him and striking savagely at his face with the flippers. The first blow knocked him half-unconscious; the second drove him into darkness.

V

ALTHOUGH HE HAD no recollection of the few seconds after his senses had dissolved, he must not have been entirely unconscious. He had gotten his two arms out from under the pinning mass and seized the flippers. Slippery as they were, he managed to keep a grip on them. He regained full consciousness just as he yanked savagely on them, so strongly that Theotormon shrieked with pain and half-rose. That was enough for Wolff. He shoved against the bulging paunch and thrust himself partly free. He bent his free right leg and kicked. Now it was Theotormon's turn to gasp for breath.

Wolff rose to his feet and kicked hard again, his shoe driving into the weakest part of the monster, his head. Theotormon, caught on the forehead, slumped back. Wolff kicked him in the jaw and then half-buried another kick in the paunch. Theotormon, the moss-green eyes glazed, fell back, his legs doubled under him.

Yet he was not out, and when Wolff advanced on him to finish his work, Theotormon kicked with a huge foot. Wolff caught the foot and so denied its full impact, but he was shoved backwards. Theotormon arose, crouched, and leaped again. Wolff also leaped forward, his right knee driving upward. It caught Theotormon on his chin, and both fell to the ground again. Wolff scrambled up, felt for his beamer, and found it was not in his holster. His brother also rose. They faced each other at a distance of six feet, both breathing heavily and just becoming aware of the pain of the blows they had taken.

Wolff's natural strength had been increased twofold by artificial means, and his bones had been toughened, without being made brittle, to match the muscular strength. However, all Lords had undergone the same treatment, so that when they engaged in physical combat among themselves, the original strength was, relatively, the same. Theotormon's body had been reshaped by Urizen, and he outweighed his brother by at least one hundred and sixty pounds. Apparently, Urizen had not increased Theotormon's power by much, since Wolff had been able to match him so far. Weight meant much in a fight, though, and it was this that Wolff had to watch for. He must not give Theotormon another chance to use it.

Theotormon, his wind having returned, growled, "I will batter you into unconsciousness again, Jadawin. And then I will carry you into the sea, dive into a cavern, and hold you while my pets eat you alive."

Wolff looked around. Vala was standing to one side and smiling very curiously. He did not waste his breath or time asking for her aid. He charged Theotormon, leaped high into the air, and kicked out with both feet. His brother had frozen for a second at the unexpected attack, then he ducked. Wolff had hoped that he would. He kicked low, but Theotormon was very fast. Wolff's shoes came down hard on his back, the shoes slipped on the wet back, and Wolff skidded down the back. He whirled even as he shot off Theotormon. The monster turned and leaped, expecting, or hoping to find Wolff flat on his back. Instead, he was caught by another kick in the jaw.

This time, Theotormon did not get up. His dark seal fur red with blood from a torn lip and gashed jaw and mashed nose, he lay breathing noisily. Wolff kicked him several times in the ribs to make sure he stayed down.

Vala applauded Wolff and said, "Well done. You

are the man I once loved—still love."

"And why didn't you help me?" he said.

"You didn't need it. I knew you'd knock that bag of blubber out of his pinhead-mind."

Wolff looked through the grass for his beamer but could not find it.

Vala did not move from where she stood. She said, "Why didn't you use your knife?"

"I would have if it had been necessary. But I want him alive. We're taking him along with us."

Her eyes widened. "In the name of Los, why?"

"Because he has certain abilities we may be able to use."

Theotormon groaned and sat up. Wolff kept an eye on him but continued his search. Finally, he said, "All right, Vala. Hand it over."

She reached within her robe and brought out the beamer. "I could kill you now."

"Do it then, but don't waste my time with idle threats. You don't scare me."

"All right. Have it then," she said fiercely. She raised the beamer and for a moment Wolff thought he had goaded her too far. After all, the Lords were proud, far too proud, and overly swift to react to insult.

But she pointed the beamer carefully at Theotormon, and a white rod of light touched the end of one flipper. Smoke curled up; burnt flesh stank. Theotormon fell backwards, his mouth open, his eyes staring.

Vala, smiling, reversed the weapon and handed it to Wolff.

He swore and said, "There was no reason but viciousness for that, Vala. Viciousness and stupidity. I tell you, he might have been the difference between death and life for us."

She walked—strolled—over to the huge wetness

and bent over to look at him. She raised the flipper, the end of which was charred.

"He's not dead—yet. You can save him, if you want to. But you'll have to cut off the flipper. It'll be cooked halfway to his shoulder."

Wolff walked away without further comment. He recruited a number of Ilmawir to help him get Theotormon on the island. Hoisted by four bladders, Theotormon rose up through a hatch. There he was pulled to one side and stretched out on the floor of a "brig." This was a cage with very light but steel-strong bars of laminated bladder-shells. Wolff did the surgery himself. After forcing a drugged drink, provided by the Ilmawir wizard, down Theotormon's throat, he examined a number of saws and other surgical tools. These were the property of the wizard, who took care of both the spiritual and physical welfare of his people.

With several saws fitted with the teeth of a sharklike fish, Wolff cut off the flipper just below the shoulder. The flesh went quickly; the bones offered enough resistance to dull two saws. The wizard thrust the red-hot end of a torch against the huge wound to seal off the blood vessels. Moreover, the wizard applied a salve to the burn, assuring Wolff that it had saved the lives of men who had been burned over half their bodies.

Vala watched the entire operation with a slight sneer. Once, her gaze met Wolff's as he looked up from his work, and she laughed. He shuddered, although she had a beautiful and striking laugh. It reminded him of a gong he had once heard while voyaging down the Guzirit river in the land of Khamshem on the third level of the planet of his own universe. It had golden notes to it, that was the only way to describe the laughter. The gong had probably been of bronze, hanging in the dark adytum of an

ancient and crumbling temple of jade and chal-
cedony, muffled by stone and the green density of the
jungle. It was bronze, but it gave forth golden vibrations. And this was how the laughter of Vala
sounded, bronze and golden and also with something
dark and smoldering in it.

She said, "He'll never be able to grow a new
flipper unless you keep peeling off the scab. You
know regeneration won't take place if there's scar
tissue."

"You let me worry about those things," he said.
"You've interfered enough."

She sniffed and went up the narrow corkscrewing
staircase to the maindeck. Wolff waited a while.
After it seemed reasonable that Theotormon was not
going to die of shock, he also went up onto the deck.
The Friiqan adoptees were being trained for their
new duties, and he watched them for a while. He
asked Dugarnn how the great gas-plants were fed,
since it seemed to him that the nutrient would weigh
much. There were at least four thousand of the bladders, each as large as the cell in a zeppelin.

Dugarnn explained. A growing bladder did not
have to be fed. But when it matured, it died. The skin
would become dry and hard but was specially treated
to preserve flexibility and expandability. New col-
onies of gas-generating bacteria were placed therein.
These had to be fed, but the amount of gas they
produced was very high in proportion to the amount
of food they needed. This was mainly the heart-stuff
of growing plants, although the bacteria could work
on fish, meat, or decaying vegetable matter.

Dugarnn left him, saying there was much work to
be done. The shadow of the moon passed, and full
daylight returned. The island began to tug harder
against the ropes. Finally, Dugarnn decided that it
was buoyant enough to cast loose. The stone anchors

were drawn up, and the ropes around the fronds cut. The island drifted past them and slowly rose. It settled at a hundred and fifty feet for a while. Then, as the gas continued to fill the bladders, it rose to five hundred feet. Dugarnn ordered the bacteria food to be reduced. He inspected the entire island, a trip which took several hours, and returned to the bridge. Wolff went down to see how Theotormon was coming along. The wizard reported that his patient was doing even better than could be expected.

Wolff climbed up a flight of steps to the top of the walls. Here he found Luvah and one of his cousins, Palamabron. The latter was a well-built and handsome man, darkest of the family. He wore a conical hat with hexagonal rim, both decorated with emerald-green owls. His cloak had a turned-up collar in back and epaulets in the shape of lions couchant. The fabric was a green shimmering stuff with a pattern of trefoils pierced with a bleeding lance. His shirt was electric-blue and piped with white skulls. A great belt of leather was bossed with gold and set with diamonds, emeralds, and topazes. His baggy pants were white-and-black striped and calf-length. The boots were of some pale soft red leather.

He made a striking and handsome figure, of which he was well aware. He nodded at Wolff's greeting, then left. Wolff, watching him, chuckled. He said, "Palamabron never did care too much for me. I would worry if he did."

"They won't do anything as long as we're on this aerial island," Luvah said. "At least, they won't unless this search takes too long. I wonder how long it will take? We could float forever over these seas and never happen across the gates."

Wolff looked at the red skies and the green-blue oceans and at the island they had left, a piece of unattached land seemingly no larger than a penny now. White birds with enormous wings and yellow curved beaks and orange-ringed eyes flew over them and gave forth shrill ululations. One settled down not far from where they stood and cocked its head and fastened an unblinking green eye upon them. Wolff remembered the ravens of his own world. Did some of these great birds have a slice of human brain within their unbird-like-sized craniums? Were they watching and listening for Urizen? Their father had some means of observing them, otherwise he would not be getting full enjoyment from this game.

"Dugarnn told me that the *abuta* is pushed always by the same wind. It takes it around and around this world of water in a spiraling path. Eventually, it covers every area."

"But the island that has the gates may always be on a different course. Always out of sight."

Wolff shrugged and said, "Then we won't find it."

"Perhaps that is the way Urizen wants it. He would like us to go mad from frustration and boredom and slit each others' throats."

"Perhaps. However, the *abuta* can change course when its people so wish. It's a slow process, but it can be done. Also . . ."

He was silent for so long that Luvah became uneasy. "Also what?"

"Our good father has placed other creatures here besides man, birds, a few animals, and fish. I understand that some of the islands, water and air alike, are populated by rather vicious flying creatures."

Vala called from below, saying that their meals were prepared. They went down to eat at one end of the chief's table. Here they heard what Dugarnn was planning. He was ready to thrust the *abuta* off course. Somewhere to the southwest was another floating island, that of their most bitter enemies, the Waerish. Now that the Ilmawir had Wolff and his beamer, they could join battle for the last time with the Waerish. It would be a glorious victory for the Ilmawir; the Waerish would be swallowed up by the ocean forever.

Wolff agreed, since there was little else he could do at that moment. He hoped that the Waerish would not be found, since he wanted to conserve the power packs of the beamer for more important matters.

The bright red days and pale red nights that followed were many and unvaried. They were, at first, however, busy for Wolff. He learned all he could about the management of the *abuta*. He studied the mores of the tribe and the idiosyncrasies of each member. The other Lords, with the exception of Vala, showed little interest in any of these. They spent their time at the bow, looking for the island that was supposed to contain the gates of Urizen. Or they complained to the *abutal* or to each other. And always one Lord was insulting another, although in a way that barely avoided an outright challenge from the insulted.

Wolff became more disgusted with them as each day passed. Except for Luvah, none was worth saving. They had an arrogance that displeased the *abutal*. Wolff warned the Lords against this many times, saying that their lives were dependent upon the natives. Should these be too antagonized, they were likely to dump the Lords overboard. His advice was taken for a while, and then the lifelong belief in their near-divinity would take hold of the Lords again.

Wolff spent much time on the bridge with Dugarnn. It was necessary to do this to smooth out the ridges of ill-feeling his brothers and cousins raised. He also went into the glider-training school, since the *abutal* could not fully give a man admiration and respect unless he had won his wings. Wolff asked Dugarnn why this was so. To Wolff, the gliders seemed more of a hindrance and unnecessary expense and trouble than anything else.

Dugarnn was astonished at the question. He groped for words, then said, "Why, it's just because . . . it is. That's all. No man is a man until he makes his first solo landing. As for your implications that gliders aren't worth the trouble, I deny those. When the day comes that we find an enemy, you will eat your words."

The next day, Wolff went up in a glider. He got into a tandem seat instruction ship, which was hauled aloft at the end of a cable borne by two great bladders. The craft rose upward until the *abuta* was a small brown oval below. Here the swifter upper winds carried them along until they were several miles ahead of the island. Then the instructor, Dugarnn, unlocked the lift mechanism. The bladders were then hauled down back to the *abuta* with a slim but strong cord, to be used again.

As Jadawin, Wolff had flown many types of craft. On Earth, he had gotten a private pilot's license qualifying him to fly single-motor craft. He had not flown for many years now, but he had not forgotten all his old skills, either. Dugarnn let him handle the controls for a while as they spiraled downwards. He tapped Wolff's shoulders and nodded approvingly, then took the controls over. The glider came in upwind, sideslipping at the last moment and landing on one side of the broad deck.

Wolff took five more lessons, during the last two of which he made the landings. On the fourth day, he soloed. Dugarnn was very impressed, saying that most students required twice that time. Wolff asked what happened if a soloing student missed the *abuta*. How could the islanders pick him up?

Dugarnn smiled and lifted his hands, palms up, and said that the unfortunate was left behind. No more was said about that, although Wolff noted that Dugarnn had insisted that the beamer be left on the island when Wolff had gone up. Wolff had placed it in the care of Luvah, whom he did not think would misuse it. Not to the extent the others would, anyway.

Thereafter, Wolff went bare-chested, as befitted a man who wore a painted *iiphtarz* upon his chest. Dugarnn insisted that Wolff also become a blood-brother. On hearing this, the other Lords scoffed.

"What, Jadawin, son of the great Lord Urizen, direct descendant of the Los himself, be brother to these painted ignorant savages? Have you no pride, brother?"

"Brother me no brother, brothers," he replied. "These people have at least not tried to slay me. That is more than I can say for any of you except Luvah. And they are not to be despised by the likes of you. They are masters of their own little worlds. You are homeless and trapped like dull-witted fat geese. So do not be so ready to scorn me or them. You would be far better off if you would condescend to make friends with them. The time may come when you will need them very much."

Theotormon, his flipper pink and half-grown out now, was squatting in the inch-deep pool. He said, "The whole accursed lot of you are doomed; long may you scream when Urizen finally closes the trap on you. But this I will say for Jadawin. He is twice the man any of you are. And I wish him luck. I wish he may get to our beloved father and exact vengeance from him, while the rest of you die horribly."

"Shut your ugly mouth, you toad!" Ariston cried. "It is bad enough to have to look at you. My stomach wrings itself out when I see you. To have to hear you, you abomination, is too much. I wish that I were in my own lovely world again and had you at my feet and in chains. Then I would make you talk, monsterling, so fast your words would be a gabble for mercy. And then I would feed you inch by inch to some special pets of my own, oh, beautiful little pets."

"And I," Theotormon said, "will pitch you over the side of this floating island some night and will laugh as I watch you flailing at the air and hear your last scream."

"Enough of this childish bickering," Vala said.

"Don't you know now that when you quarrel among yourselves, you delight the heart of our father? He would love to see you tear each other apart."

"Vala is right," Wolff said. "You call yourselves Lords, makers and rulers of entire universes. Yet you behave like spoiled, and evil, brats. If you hate each other, remember that the one who taught you this horrible hatred, and who now has set the stage for your death, still lives. He must die. If we have to die ourselves in making sure of his death, so be it. But at least try to live with dignity and so dignify your deaths."

Suddenly, Ariston strode towards Wolff. His face was red, and his mouth was twisted. He towered over Wolff, though he was not as broad. He waved his arms, and the saffron robes, set with scarlet and green imbrications, flapped.

"I have put up with enough from you, detested brother!" he howled. "Your insults and your insinuations that you are better than us now because you have become less than us—one of those animals—have enraged me. I hate you as I have always hated you, hated you far more than the others. You are nothing—a . . . a . . . foundling!"

With this insult, the worst the Lords could conceive, for they could think of nothing worse than not to be of the true lineage of Lords, he began to draw his knife. Wolff bent his knees, ready to fight if he had to but hoping he would not. It would look very bad for the Lords if they brawled in front of the *abutal*.

At that moment, a cry arose from the gondola on the prow of the island. Drums began to beat, and the *abutal* dropped what they were doing. Wolff caught hold of a man running by and asked what the alarm was about.

The man pointed to the left, indicating something in the sky. Wolff turned to see an object, dark and fuzzy against the red dome of the sky.

VI

EVEN AS WOLFF ran towards the bridge, another object appeared. Before he had reached the gondola, he saw two more. They made him prickle with uneasiness and a sense of strangeness. He could not identify the reason for this at first. But before he reached the gondola, he knew. The objects were not drifting with the wind but were coming in at right angles to it. Something was propelling them.

On the bridge, Dugarnn told Wolff what he wanted of him. He was to stay by his side until ordered otherwise. As for the other Lords, now was the time for them to earn their keep. Dugarnn had heard them boasting of their prowess. Let them put their swords where their mouths were—or words to that effect.

Communication on the island-surface during a battle was by drum. Orders to those inside the island, stationed on the ports on the sides or the hatches at the bottom, were transmitted by another means. Throughout the *abuta* was a network of thin narrow pipes. These were fashioned from the bones of the *girrel* fish, and had the property of transmitting sound quite well. The *abutal* could use voice over the girrel-bones up to seventy-five feet. Past this distance, a code was rapped out by a tiny hammer.

Wolff watched Dugarnn issue orders, which were performed swiftly by the well-trained people. Even children were carrying out duties within their capabilities, and so relieving adults for more difficult and dangerous posts. To Vala, who had come up to the bridge, Wolff said, "We so-called divine Lords could learn much about cooperation from these so-called savages."

"No doubt," Vala replied. She looked out across

the oceans and said, "There are six now. What are they?"

"Dugarnn mentioned the Nichiddor, but he had no time to tell me what they are. Be patient. We'll know soon enough. Too soon, I suspect."

The gliders had been fastened to the lift-bladders. The pilots got into the cockpits while the "ground" crews fitted the explosive bladder-bombs to the wings. Then the wizard, clad in robes and a mask, passed along the gliders. He carried a double-ankh with which he blessed the pilots and their craft. Between each glider, he stopped to shake the double-ankh at the *ufo* and hurl maledictions. Dugarnn became impatient but dared not hurry the wizard. As soon as the last of the twenty airmen had been touched by the ankh and prayed over, Dugarnn gave the signal. The bladders with their white-winged cargoes were released. They soared up and up until they had attained a height of a thousand feet above the island.

Dugarnn said, "They'll release themselves as soon as the Nichiddor nests get within range. Los guard them, since few will get through. But if the nests can be destroyed . . ."

"There are eight now," Wolff said. The nearest was a half-mile away. Ball-shaped, it had a diameter of about three hundred yards. The fuzzy appearance had been caused by the many uneven projections of plants. These grew out to conceal the gas-bladders that formed irregular concentric rings. On the surface of the spheroid nest were hundreds of tiny figures. An aerial dung-ball, Wolff thought.

Dugarnn pointed above him, and Wolff saw a number of small dark objects. "Scouts," Dugarnn said. "The Nichiddor won't attack until the scouts report to them."

"Who are the Nichiddor?"

"There's one now, coming down to take a close look."

The wings were black-feathered and had a spread of at least fifty feet. They sprouted out from the five-foot wide shoulders, below which was a hairless human torso. The breast-bone projected several feet and under it was the abdomen with a human navel. The legs were thin and ended in huge feet that were mainly clawlike toes. A long black feathered tail spread out behind it. The face was human except for the nose. This extended like an elephant's proboscis for several feet and was as flexible. As the Nichiddor swept over them, it raised the proboscis and trumpeted shrilly.

Dugarnn glanced at Wolff's beamer. Wolff shook his head and said, "I'd rather they didn't know yet what they're up against. My supply of charges is limited. I want to wait until I can get a number with a single shot."

He watched the Nichiddor flap heavily away towards the nearest nest. The creatures were undoubtedly the work of Urizen, who had placed them here for his own amusement. They must be human beings—although not necessarily Lords—he had transmuted in the laboratory. They could have been abducted from other worlds then his; some might even be descended from Earthmen. Now they lived a strange life beneath red skies and a dark moon, born and raised on an aerial nest that drifted with the winds of this landless world. They lived largely on fish, which they caught as an osprey catches fish, with their talons. But when they came across a surface or air-island, they killed to eat raw human flesh.

By now Wolff could see why the nests were going against the wind. The hundreds of Nichiddors on it had gripped the plants in their talons and were flapping their wings in unison. The foul chariot of the skies was drawn by as strange birds as ever existed.

When the nest had come within a quarter-mile, the wings stopped beating. Now the other nests drew up slowly. Two settled downwards; from these the Nichiddor would attack the bottom of the island. Two others veered around behind the island and then came on the other side. Dugarnn waited calmly until the Nichiddor had set their attack pattern.

Wolff asked him why he did not order the gliders to attack.

"If they were released before the main body of Nichiddor came at us," Dugarnn said, "every Nichiddor would rise to bar the way. The gliders could not possibly get through them. But with only a small number of Nichiddor attacking the gliders, we have a chance of getting through to the nests. At least, that has been my experience so far."

"Wouldn't it be wisest, from the Nichiddors' viewpoint, to eliminate the gliders first?" Wolff asked.

Dugarnn shrugged and said, "You'd think so. But they never do what seems to me the most strategic thing. It's my theory that, being deprived of hands, the Nichiddor have suffered a lessening of intelligence. It's true they can manipulate objects to some extent with their feet and their trunks, but they're far less manual than we.

"Then again, I could be wrong. Perhaps the Nichiddor derive a certain pleasure from giving the gliders a fighting chance. Or perhaps they are as arrogant as sea-eagles, which will attack a shark that outweighs them by a thousand pounds, a vicious creature that an eagle cannot possibly kill or, if it could, would not be able to carry off to some surface island."

The wind carried to the *abuta* the gabble of hundreds of voices and the trumpeting of hundreds of proboscises. Suddenly, there was a silence. Dugarnn froze, but his eyes were busy. Slowly, he raised his hand. A warrior standing near him held a bladder in his hand. By him was a bowl-shaped stone with some hot coals. He held his gaze upon his chief.

The silence was broken with the united scream of Nichiddor through their snaky noses. There was a clap as of thunder as they launched themselves from the nests and brought their wings together in the first beat. Dugarnn dropped his hand. The warrior dipped the short fuse of the bladder into the fire and then released it. It soared upwards to fifty feet and exploded.

The gliders dropped from their lifts, each towards the nest appointed to it. Wolff looked at the dark hordes advancing and lost some of his confidence in his beamer. Yet, the Ilmawir had beaten off attacks by the Nichiddor before—although with great loss. But never before had eight nests ringed the *abuta*.

A great-winged white bird passed overhead. Its cry came down to him, and he wondered if this could be an eye of Urizen. Was his father watching through the eyes and brains of these birds? If so, he was going to see a spectacle that would delight his bloody heart.

The Nichiddor, so thick they were a brown and black cloud, surrounded the island. Just out of bow-range, they stopped advancing and began to fly around the island. Around and around they flew, in an ever-diminishing circle. The Ilmawir archers, all males, waited for their chief to signal to fire. The women were armed with slings and stones, and they also waited.

Dugarnn, knowing that it would weaken them to spread out his people along the top of the walls, had concentrated them at the prow. There was nothing to prevent the Nichiddor from landing at the far end. However, they did not settle down there. They hated to walk on their weak legs.

Wolff looked out at the gliders. Some had dropped below his line of vision to attack the two nests below the underside. The others were coming down swiftly in a steep glide. A number of Nichiddor rose from the nest to meet them.

Two fliers passed over the nearest nest. Small objects, trailing smoke, dropped from them and fell on the nests. Females, flapping their wings, scrambled towards them. Then, there was an explosion. Smoke and fire billowed out. Another explosion followed.

The two gliders pulled up sharply. Carried upward by the momentum of their steep dives, they turned and came back for another and final pass. Again, their bombs hit. Fire spread through the dry plants and caught and enfolded some of the giant gas-cells. The females screamed so loudly they could be heard even above the wing-beatings and trumpetings of the circling horde. They rose from the burning nest, their infants clutched in their toes. The entire nest blew apart, catching some of the females, burning them in flight or hurling them head over heels. Infants dropped towards the sea below, their short wings ineffectively flapping.

Wolff saw one mother fold her wings and drop like a fish-hawk towards her infant. She caught it, beat her wings, and lifted slowly towards an untouched nest.

Two nest, burning and exploding, spun towards the ocean. By then several hundreds of males had detached themselves from the ring around the island. They flew after the gliders, which by now were far down, headed towards a landing on the waves.

The nests on a level with the island were out of range of his beamer. It was possible the two below might not be. Wolff told Dugarnn what he meant to

do and went down a fifty-foot winding staircase to a
hatch at its bottom. The nests there had risen close,
and he caught both of them with a sweep of the full
power of the beamer. They blew up with such vio-
lence that he was lifted and almost knocked off the
platform. Smoke poured up through the hatch. Then,
as it cleared away, he saw the flaming pieces of
vegetation falling. The bodies of the children and
females plummeted into the sea.

The male warriors from the nests were trying to get
through the bottom hatches. Wolff put the beamer on
half-power and cleared the area. Then he ran along
the gangplank, stopping at every hatch to fire again.
He accounted for at least a hundred attackers. Some
had gotten through the defending *abutal* at the
hatches at the far end. It took him a while to kill
these, since he had to be careful not to touch the
many great bladders. Even though he slew thirty, he
could not get them all. The island was too large for
him to cover all the bottom area.

By the time he climbed back up to the hatch, he
found that the Nichiddor had launched their mass
attack. This end of the island was a swirling, screech-
ing, shouting, screaming mob. There were bodies
everywhere.

The archers and slingers had taken a heavy toll of
the first wave and a lighter toll of the second. Then
the Nichiddor were upon them, and the battle became a melee. Although the winged men had no
weapons other than their wings and feet, these were
powerful. With a sweep of a wing, a Nichiddor could
knock down an Ilmawir. He could then leap upon his
stunned and bruised foe and tear at him with the
heavy hooked clawlike toenails. The *abutal* de-
fended themselves with spears, swords which were
flat blades lined with shark's teeth, and knives
formed from a bamboolike surface plant.

Wolff methodically set about to kill all those in the neighborhood of the maindeck. The Lords had made a compact group, all facing outwards and slashing with their swords. Wolff took careful aim and slew the Nichiddor pressing them. A shadow fell on him, and he fell on his back and fired upwards. Two Nichiddor struck the deck on each side of him, the wing of one buffeting him. It covered him like a banner and stank of fish. He crawled out from under just in time to shoot two that had forced Dugarnn back against the wall. Dugarnn's wife lay near him, her spear stuck in a winged man's belly. Her face and breasts were ripped into shreds, and the Nichiddor who had done it was tearing out her belly. He fell backwards, his claws caught in her entrails, as Wolff shot him from behind.

For the next minute, it was near-death for him. At least two dozen Nichiddor came at him from all sides and from above. He spun like a top, using the beam as a spray, around him and in the air. The corpses, half-severed, smoking, stinking, piled up around him. Then he was over them, out in the open, on the fringes of the eddying battle. He shot everywhere and usually hit his target, though twice an *abutal* was borne by the thrust of the fight into the beam. This could not be helped; he was lucky that he had not hit more.

The Ilmawir, despite a fierce resistance, had lost half their numbers. Even with Wolff's help, they were being defeated. The Nichiddor, despite casualties that should have made them retreat, refused to stop. They were intent on extermination of their foe, even if it meant near-extermination for them.

Wolff cleared the attackers around the Lords again. They were all on their feet and swinging their swords, although covered with blood. Wolff called to them to form around him. While they kept off the winged men, he would shoot over them. He stood upon a pile of Nichiddor, his feet braced on the slippery corpses, and coolly resumed firing. Suddenly, he realized that he was down to his last two power packs. He had hoped to save some for Urizen's stronghold, but there was nothing he could do to conserve them now. If he did not use the beamer, he and all that fought with him would die.

Vala, standing just in front of him, yelled. He looked upward where she was pointing. A dark object spanned the skies: a black comet. It had appeared while all were intent upon the fight.

The *abutal* near them also looked up. They gave a cry of despair and threw down their weapons. Ignoring the winged men, they ran towards the nearest hatches. The Nichiddor, after searching the skies for the cause of the panic, also reacted with terror. They launched themselves into the air to get to the nests or to escape to the protecting underside of the island.

Wolff did not throw down his beamer, but he was as frenzied as the others in their attempt to get to the closest cover. Dugarnn had told him of the black comets that occasionally visited the space above this planet. He had warned of that which always accompanied the comet.

As Wolff raced towards a hatch, there were small whistling noises around him. Holes appeared in the foliage of the walls; little curls of smoke rose from the sheathing of the maindeck. A Nichiddor, ten feet up, flapping his fifty-foot wings frantically, screamed. He fell to the deck, his skin pierced in several places, smoke coming from one wing. Another and another winged man dropped, and with them some *abutal*. The corpses jerked with the impact of the tiny drops.

Wolff's beamer was knocked out of his hand by the blow of a drop of quicksilver. He stooped and picked it up and resumed his run. For a moment, he could not get into the hatchway because of the Lords jammed before it. They fought each other, cursed, and cried to Los. Some even cried out for their father, Urizen, or their long-dead mother.

For one wild second, Wolff thought of clearing the way for him with the beamer. It was exactly what any of them, with the possible exception of Luvah, would have done. To stay out here was to be dead. Every bit of time counted.

Then whoever was the cause of the pile-up got through, and the others clawed and bit and scratched their way in.

Wolff went through the hatch in a dive, headfirst. Something touched his pants. His calf burned. There was a splashing noise, and hot mercury clung to the back of his head. He fell past the shallow ladder and hit the floor with his two hands, dropping the beamer before he hit. He absorbed most of the shock with his bent arms and then rolled over. He brought up against Palamabron, who was just starting down the second ladder. Palamabron yelled and pitched forward. Wolff, looking down the well, saw Palamabron on top of a pile of Lords. All were shouting and cursing. None, however, seemed to be hurt badly.

At another time Wolff would have laughed. Now he was too concerned with scraping the globules of hot mercury from his hair. He examined his leg to make sure that the hit there had only been glancing. Then he went on down the steps. It was best to get as far below as possible. If this were a heavy and steady mercury-drop shower, the entire upper decks could be destroyed. If the big gas-bladders were penetrated, good-bye forever to all.

VII

VALA GREETED HIM in the twilight of a gangplank by a spheroid cell. She was laughing. Her laughter was not hysteria but genuine amusement. He was sure that if there were enough light, he would be able to see her eyes shining with mirth.

"I'm glad that you find this funny," he said. He was covered with Nichiddor blood, which was rapidly being carried off by his heavy sweating, and he was shaking. "You were always a strange one, Vala. Even as a child, you loved teasing the rest of us and playing cruel jokes upon us. And as a woman, you loved blood and suffering—in others—more than you loved love."

"So I am a true Lord," she said. "My father's daughter. And, I might add, my brother's sister. You were just like me, dear Jadawin, before you became the namby-pamby human Wolff, the degenerate half-Earthling."

She came closer, and, lowering her voice, said, "It has been a long time since I have had a man, Jadawin. And you have not touched a woman since you came through the gate. Yet I know that you are like a he-goat, brother, and that you begin to suffer when a day passes without taking a woman to bed. Can you put aside your so-evident loathing of me—which I do not understand—and go with me now? There are a hundred hiding places in this island, dark and warm and private places where no one will disturb us. I ask you, though my pride is great."

She spoke truly. He was an exceedingly strong and vigorous man. Now he felt longing come upon him, a longing that he had put aside every day by constant activity. When night came and he went to bed, he had bent his mind to plots against his father, trying to foresee a thousand contingencies and the best way to dispose of them.

"First the blood-feast and then the lust-dessert," he said. "It's not I who rouses you but the thrust of the blade and the spurt of blood."

"Both do," she said. She held out her hand to him. "Come with me."

He shook his head. "No. And I want to hear no more of this. The subject is forever dead."

She snarled, "As you will soon be. No one can . . ."

Vala turned and walked away, and when he next saw her, she was talking earnestly to Palamabron. After a while, the two walked off into the dimness of a corridor.

He thought for a moment of ordering them back. They were in effect deserting their posts. The danger from the Nichiddor seemed to be over, but if the mercury shower became heavier, the island could be badly crippled or destroyed.

He shrugged and turned away. After all, he had no delegated authority. The cooperation among the Lords was only a spoken agreement; there was no formal agreement of organization with a system of punishments. Also, if he tried to interfere, he would be accused of doing so because of jealousy. The charge would not be entirely baseless. He did feel a pang at seeing Vala go off with another man. And this was a measure of what he had once felt for her, that after five hundred years and what she had tried to do to him, he should care even the fraction of a bit.

He said to Dugarnn, "How long does a shower last?"

"About a half-hour," the chief replied. "The drops are carried along with the black comets. The laughter of Urizen, we call them, since he must have created them. Urizen is a cruel and bloody god who rejoices in the sufferings of his people.''

Dugarnn did not have exactly the same attitude towards Urizen that the Lords did. In the course of the many thousands of years since the descendants of the trapped Lords had been here, the name of Urizen had become that of the evil god in the *abutal* pantheon. Dugarnn had no true idea of the universe in which he was born. To him, this world was *the* world, the only one. The Lords were demigods, sons and daughters of Urizen by mortal women. The Lords were mortal, too, though extraordinarily powerful.

There was an explosion, and Wolff feared for a moment that one of the gas-bladders at the far end of the island had been penetrated. One of the *abutal* said that a Nichiddor nest had gone up. Less protected then the island, it had received a concentration of drops, one bladder had blown up another, and in the chain reaction the whole nest was hurled apart.

Wolff went over to where Theotormon crouched in a corner. His brother looked up at him with hate and misery. He turned his head away when Wolff spoke to him. After a while, as Wolff squatted quietly by him, Theotormon began to fidget. He finally looked at Wolff and said, ''Father told me that there are four planets that revolve in orbit about a central fifth. This is Appirmatzum, the planet on which is his stronghold. Each planet is about the size of this one, and all are separated from Appirmatzum by only twenty thousand miles. This universe is not a recent one. It was created as one of a series by our father at least fifteen thousand years ago. They were kept hidden, their gates only being activated when Father wished to enter or leave one. Thus, the scanners failed to detect them.''

''Then that is why I've seen only three of the

planets," Wolff said. "The outer ones are at the corners of an equilateral quadrangle. The planet opposite is always hidden by Appirmatzum."

He did not wonder at the forces which enabled such large bodies to be so relatively close and yet stay in undeviating paths. The science of the Lords was beyond his comprehension—as a matter of fact, it was beyond the understanding of any of the Lords. They had inherited and used a power the principles of which they no longer understood. They did not care to understand. It was enough that they could use the powers.

This very lack of knowledge of principles made the Lords so vulnerable at times. Each only had so many weapons and machines. If any were destroyed, lost, or stolen, a Lord could only replace them by stealing them from other Lords—if there were any still in existence. And the defenses they set up against other Lords always had holes in them, no matter how impregnable the defenses seemed. The vital thing was to live long enough while attacking to find these holes. So, no matter how powerless the group seemed at the moment, Wolff had hopes that he could win.

While waiting for the mercury shower to cease, he had time to think. From some corner of his mind came an irrelevancy that had been bothering him for a long long time. It had nothing to do with the present situation. It might have been sent by the unconscious to keep him from worrying about Chryseis, for whom he could do nothing at all at this moment.

The names of his father, brothers, sisters, and cousins had made him wonder ever since he had regained his memory of his life as Jadawin, Lord of the World of Tiers. Urizen, Vala, Luvah, Anana, Theotormon, Palamabron, Enion, Ariston, Tharmas, Rintrah, these were the names of the vast and dark cosmogens found in William Blake's Didactic and Symbolical Works. It was no coincidence that they were the same. Of that Wolff was convinced. But how had the mystical English poet come across them? Had he known a dispossessed Lord, wandering on Earth, who had told him of the Lords for some reason? It was possible. And Blake must have used some of the Lord's story as a basis for his apocalyptic poetry. But the story had been very much distorted by Blake.

Some day, if Wolff got out of this trap, he would do some research on Earth and also among those Lords who would let him get close enough to them to talk.

The pounding of the quicksilver stopped. After waiting for half an hour to make sure that the storm was all over, the islanders went back upon the maindeck. The floor was broken up, pitted, and scorched. The walls had been pierced so many times that the roots and leaves were rags of vegetation. The gondola had been hit by an especially heavy concentration and was a wreck. Tiny globules of mercury lay all over the deck.

Theotormon said, "The mercury shower can't be compared to a meteor shower. The drops are only traveling about a hundred miles an hour when they hit the atmosphere, and they are considerably slowed up and broken up before they reach the surface. Yet . . ."

He waved a flipper to indicate the damage.

Wolff looked out over the sea. The surviving nests were drifting slowly away. The winged men had enough problems of their own without resuming the attack. One nest was so overburdened with refugees from others that it was losing altitude.

Dugarnn was sad. He had lost so many people that it would be very difficult to maneuver the island and impossible to defend it against another attack. Now they would drift helplessly around and around the world. Not until the children had grown up would they become powerful again. It was unlikely that the island would be left alone long enough for the children to become adults.

"My people are doomed," he said.

"Not as long as you keep fighting," Wolff said. "After all, you can avoid battle with other *abutal* islands and with the surface islands. You told me that the only reason two *abuta* get together for a conflict is that both maneuver to approach each other. You can quit doing that. And the Nichiddor are rare. This is the first time in fifteen years that you have met a cluster of nests."

"What! Run away from a fight!" Dugarnn said. His mouth hung open. "That . . . that's unthinkable. We would be cowards. Our names would be a scornword in the mouths of our enemies."

"That's a lot of nonsense," Wolff said. "The other *abutal* can't even get close enough to identify you unless you let them. But that's up to you. Die because you can't change your ways, if that's what you want."

Wolff was busy helping to clean up the island. The dead and wounded Nichiddor were dumped overboard. The dead *abutal* were given a long burial ceremony, officiated over by Dugarnn, since the wizard had had his head twisted off during the battle. Then the bodies were slipped over the side and received by the sea.

Days and nights drifted by as slowly as the wind-driven island. Wolff spent much time observing the great brown spheres of the other planets. Appirmatzum was only twenty thousand miles away. So near and yet so far. It might as well be a million miles. Or was it truly so impossible to get there? A plan began to form, a plan so fantastic that he almost abandoned it. But, if he could get the materials, he might, just might, carry it out.

The *abuta* passed over the polar area, the surface of which looked just like the others. Twice, they saw enemy islands at a distance. When these began to work their way towards Dugarnn's island, Dugarnn sadly ordered his island to flee. The banks of gas-bladders on one side were operated to give the island a slow lateral thrust, and the distance between the two was kept equal. After a while, the enemy gave up, having used up as much gas in his bladders as he dared.

Dugarnn explained that the maneuvers which brought two *abuta* into battle-conflict sometimes took as much as five days.

"I've never seen people so anxious to die," was Wolff's only comment.

One day, when it seemed to all the Lords that they would drift above the featureless waters forever, a lookout gave a cry that brought them running.

"The Mother of All Islands!" he shouted. "Dead ahead! The Mother of Islands!"

If this was the mother of islands, then her babies must be small indeed. From three thousand feet, Wolff could span the floating mass from shore to shore with one sweep of the eye. It was not more than thirty miles wide at the broadest and twelve miles long. But most things are relative, and on this world it was a continent.

There were bays and inlets and even broken spaces that formed lakes of sea-water. At various times, some force, perhaps collision with other islands, had crumpled up parts of the island. These formed hills. And it was on top of one of the hills that Wolff saw the gates.

There were two, hexagons of some self-illumi-
nated metal, each huge as the open end of a zeppelin
hangar.

Wolff hurried to notify Dugarnn. The commander
was aware of the gates and was barking out orders. A
long time ago, he had promised Wolff that when the
gates were found, he would terminate the agreement.
Wolff and the beamer and the Lords could leave the
abuta.

There was not near enough time to valve off gas to
lower the island. Before the desired altitude could be
reached, the *abuta* would have drifted far past the
Mitza, the mother. So the Lords hastened to the
lowest deck, where jump-bladder harnesses were
ready for them. They strapped the belts around their
shoulders, chests, and legs and then were towed to
the hatch. Dugarnn and the *abutal* crowded around
them to say farewell. They said no words of good-bye
to any of the Lords but Wolff and Luvah. These two
they kissed, and they pressed the flower of the young
gas-plant in their hands. Wolff said farewell and
stepped through the hatch. He fell as swiftly as a man
below an open parachute. The other Lords followed
him. There was an open space among the fronds in
which he tried to land, but he miscalculated the wind.
He crashed into the top of a frond, which bent beneath him and so broke his fall. The others also made
good landings, though some were bruised. Theotormon had an extra large jump-harness because of his
four hundred and fifty pounds, but he came down
faster than the others anyway. His rubbery legs bent
under him; he rolled; and he was up on his feet,
squawking because he had banged his head.

Wolff waited until they were recovered. He waved
at the Ilmawir, who were peering down at him from
the hatches. Then the island passed on and presently
was out of their sight. The Lords made their way

through the jungle towards the hill. They were alert, since they had seen many native villages from the *abuta*. But they came to the hill-gates without seeing the aborigines and presently were standing before the towering hexagons.

"Why two?" Palamabron said.

Vala said, "That is another of our father's riddles, I'm sure. One gate must lead to his palace on Appirmatzum. The other, who knows where?"

"But how will we know?" Palamabron said.

"Stupid!" Vala said. "We won't know until we go through one or the other."

Wolff smiled slightly. Ever since she had gone off with Palamabron, she had treated him with even more contempt and scorn than the others. Palamabron was bewildered by this. Evidently, he had been expecting some sort of gratitude.

Wolff said, "We should all go through the same one. It won't be wise to split up our forces. Wrong one or right one, we must be united."

Palamabron said, "You are right, brother. Besides, if we split, and one group were to get into Urizen's stronghold and kill him, then that group would have control. And they would betray the second group."

"That is not why I think we should stay together," Wolff said. "But you have a good point."

"On top of his head," Vala said. "Palamabron is no more of a thinker than he is a lover."

Palamabron reddened, and he put his hand upon the hilt of his sword. "I am through swallowing your insults, you vixen in heat," he said. "One more, and your head will roll off your shoulders."

"We have enough fighting ahead of us," Wolff said. "Save your fury for that which lies on the other side of one of those gates."

He saw a movement in the bushes a hundred yards

away. Presently, a face showed. A native was watching them. Wolff wondered if any of the natives had tried to go through the gates. If one had, his disappearance would have terrified the others. Possibly, this area was tabu.

He was interested in the natives' reactions, because he considered that they might be of some help, someday. Just now, he did not have time or did not wish to take time. Chryseis was in Urizen's stronghold, and every minute there must be agony. It might not be agony only of spirit; she could be tormented physically by his father.

He shuddered and tried to put out of his mind the pictures that this thought painted. One thing at a time.

He looked at the others. They were watching him intently. Although they would have strongly denied it, they regarded him as a leader. He was not the oldest brother and one of his cousins was older. But he had taken immediate and forceful measures whenever any crisis had come up on this world. And he had the beamer. Moreover, they seemed to detect something different in him, a dimension that they lacked—although they would have denied this, too. His experience as Robert Wolff, the Earthman, had given him a grip upon matters that they had always considered too mundane to bother with. Insulated from hard labor, from having to deal with things at a primitive level, they felt lost. Once they had been makers and semidivine rulers of their own private universes. Now they were no better—perhaps not as good—as the savages they so despised. Jadawin—or Wolff, as they were beginning to call him—was a man who knew his way around in a world of savages.

Wolff said, "It's one fate or the other. A case of eenie meenie minie moe."

"And what barbaric language is that?" Vala said.

"Earth type. I'll tell you what. Vala is the only woman here . . ."

"But more of a man than most of you," Vala said.

". . . so why don't we let her pick out which one we enter? It's as good a method as any for choosing."

"That bitch never did anything right in her life," Palamabron said. "But I say, let her designate the gate. Then we won't go wrong if we enter the one she doesn't choose."

"Do what you like," Vala said. "But I say—that one."

She pointed at the right-hand hexagon.

"Very well," Wolff said. "Since I have the beamer, I'll go first. I don't know what's on the other side. Rather, I know what is there—death—but I don't know what form it'll take. Before I go, I'd like to say this. There was a time, brothers, cousins, sister, when we loved each other. Our mother lived then, and we were happy with her. We were in awe of our father, the gloomy, remote, forbidding Urizen. But we did not hate him. Then our mother died. How she died, we still don't know. I think, as some of you do, that Urizen killed our mother. It was only three days after she died that he took to wife Araga, the Lord of her own world, and so united his domain with hers.

"Whoever murdered our mother, we know what happened after that. We found out that Urizen was beginning to be sorry that he had children. He was one of the very few Lords to have children being raised as Lords. The Lords are dying out; they are paying for their immortality, so-called, and for their power, with gradual extinction. They have also paid with the loss of that one thing that makes life worthwhile: love."

"Love!" said Vala. She laughed, and the others joined her. Luvah half-smiled, but he did not laugh.

"You sound like a pack of hyenas," Wolff said. "Hyenas are carrion-eaters, powerful, nasty, vicious brutes, whose stench and habits make them despised and hated everywhere. However, they do serve a useful function, which is more than I can say for you.

" 'Love,' I said. And I repeat it again. The word means nothing to you; it has been too many thousands of years since you felt it. And I doubt that any of you felt it very strongly then. Anyway, as I was saying, we found out that Urizen was considering doing away with us. Or at least disowning us and driving us out to live with the aborigines on a planet in one of his universes, a world which he intended to make gateless so we could never strike back at him. We fled. He came after us and tried to kill us. We got away, and we killed other Lords and took over their worlds.

"Then we forgot we were brothers and sisters and cousins and became true Lords. Hateful, scheming, jealous, possessive. Murderers, cruel alike to each other and to the miserable beings who populated our worlds."

"Enough of this, brother," Vala said. "What are you getting at?"

Wolff sighed. He was wasting his breath.

"I was going to say that perhaps Urizen has done us a favor without meaning to. Perhaps we could somehow find it in ourselves to resurrect the childhood love, to act as brothers should. We . . ."

He stopped. Their faces were like those of stone idols. Time could break them, but love would never soften them.

He turned and stepped through the right-hand gate.

VIII

HIS FEET SLID out from under him, and he fell on his side. He caught a glimpse of smooth glassy surfaces as he slid down the hill on top of which the gate was set. The stuff on which he raced downhill was dry and slippery, although it gave an impression of oiliness. No matter how he tried to dig his heels in, how strongly he placed the flats of his hands against the stuff to brake himself, he sped on down. It was like being on ice.

He shot on, gaining speed. Throwing himself over with a convulsive twist, he managed to face the direction in which, willynilly, he was going. Ahead was a gentling of the slope, and when he reached it his velocity slowed somewhat. Still, he was going at least sixty miles an hour with no way of stopping himself. His head was raised to keep his face from being burned and his hands were upheld. By then his clothes should have been burned off him, and his flesh should have been crisped and unraveling from the friction, but he sped on with only a slight feeling of warmth.

The skies were purple, and just above the edge of the horizon, the arc of a moon—he thought it was a moon—was showing. The arc was a deeper purple than the skies. He was not inside any Lord's palace; he was on another planet. Judging from the distance of the horizon, this planet was about the size of the one he had just left. In fact, he was sure that it was one of the bodies that he had seen in the skies from the surface of the waterworld.

Urizen had tricked them. He had set up the gate through which they had gone to jump them to one of the bodies circling about Appirmatzum. The other gate back on the waterworld might have led to Urizen's world. Or, it might have led to here also. There was no way of knowing now.

Whichever way the other entrance presented, it was too late to do anything about it. He was caught helplessly in one of his father's jokes. A practical joke, if you could consider death as practical.

He had traveled perhaps two miles when the incline began to turn upwards. Within a half-mile, he was slowed down to what seemed a thirty-mile an hour velocity, although it was difficult to tell with the few references he had. Off to his right, at a long distance, were a number of peculiar-looking trees. Not knowing how tall they were or how far away, he could not determine just how fast he was traveling.

And then, just as he slowed down to about ten miles an hour, and the incline sloped sharply upwards, he rose over its edge. He was in the air, out over the lip of the rise, beyond the edge of a precipice. He fell, unable to hold back a scream. Below him, forty or fifty feet, was a one hundred foot wide stream of water. The other side was blocked off by a wall of the same vitreous substance on which he had slid.

He dropped into the canyon, kicking to maintain an upright position so he could hit the water feet-first. The water was not as far away as he had thought, however, being only thirty-five feet down. He struck with his feet and plunged into tepid waters. He went on down, down, then began to swim upwards. The current carried him on swiftly between the canyon walls and took him around a bend. Just before he was carried around it, he saw a Lord hit the surface and another halfway down the wall.

Then the canyon opened out, and the river broadened. He was sliding and bumping over rapids. Fortunately, the rocks were smooth and slick, vitreous also. He escaped cuts but did suffer some bruises. Once past the rapids, he found that the current had slowed. He swam to the shore, which led up gently from the water. But he could not keep a handhold on the land and slid back into the river.

There was nothing to do but swim along the shoreline and hope that eventually he would find a place which would enable him to scramble onto the land. His clothes and the bow and arrows and knife and beamer weighed him down. As long as he could, he resisted the need to abandon them. When he began to tire, he slipped off the bow and quiver. Later, he unstrapped his belt and holster and scabbard. These he dropped into the water, but slipped the beamer and his knife inside his pants. After a while, he rid himself of the knife.

Now and then, he looked back. Eight heads were bobbing up and down. All had survived so far, but if the banks continued to resist grasping, they would all soon be drowned. All except Theotormon. He could outswim and outfloat them all, even with one flipper only half-grown out.

It was then that Wolff got an idea. He swam against the current, although the effort took more strength than he could afford. He swam until Luvah and Vala and Tharmas were close to him. Then he yelled at them to also swim against the current, if they wished to be saved.

Presently Theotormon's huge, oily, blue-black bulk was beside him. Behind him came Ariston, Enion, and Rintrah. Last of all, the most boastful but the most fearful to enter the gate, was Palamabron. His face was white, and he was breathing even more heavily than the rest.

"Save me, brother!" he cried. "I can't go on much longer. I will die."

"Save your breath," Wolff said. To Theotormon,

he said, "We have need of you, brother. Now you, the once-despised, can help us. Without you, we shall all drown."

Theotørmon, swimming easily against the current, chuckled. He said, "Why should I? You all spit on me; you say I make you sick."

"I have never spit upon you," Wolff said. "Nor have I said you sicken me. And it was I who insisted that you come with us. I did so because I knew that we would need you. There are things you can do with that body that we cannot. It is ironic that Urizen, who set this trap, and who also transformed you into a sea-thing, prepared you to survive in his trap. He unwittingly gave you the means to escape and so to help us escape."

It was a long speech under the circumstances and left him winded. Nevertheless, he had to praise Theotormon; otherwise, he would leave them to die and laugh while doing so.

Theotormon said, "You mean Urizen outwitted himself?"

Wolff nodded.

"And how can I escape from this?" Theotormon said.

"You are swift and strong as a seal in the water. You can propel yourself so swiftly that you can shoot through the water and on up onto the bank. You can also shove us, one by one, onto the bank. I know that you can do this."

Theotormon grinned slyly. "And why should I push you to safety?"

"If you don't, you'll be left alone on this strange world," Wolff said. "You can live for a while. But you'll be lonely. I doubt that there's anyone here you can talk to. Moreover, if we're to get off this world, we have to find the gates which will lead us off. Can you do this alone? Once on land, you'll need us."

"To hell with you!" Theotormon screamed. He upended and disappeared beneath the surface.

"Theotormon!" Wolff called.

The others echoed his call. They treaded water and looked despairingly at each other. There was nothing of the haughty Lord in their faces now.

Suddenly, Vala screamed. She threw her hands up into the air and went under. So swiftly she went, she must have been pulled under.

A few seconds passed. Then Theotormon's oily blue-black head appeared and a moment later Vala's red hair. Her brother's long toes were entangled in her hair, her head held by the foot.

"Say you're sorry!" Theotormon shouted. "Apologize! Tell me I'm not a loathsome mass of blubber! Tell me I'm beautiful! Promise to love me as you did Palamabron on the island!"

She tore her hair loose, leaving some dark red strands between his toes. She screamed, "I'll kill you, you blotch! I'm a long way from dying yet! And if I were, I'd go gladly to my death rather than make up to you!"

His eyes wide, Theotormon paddled away from her with his feet. He turned to Wolff and said, "See! Why should I save her or any of you? You would still hate me, just as I would hate you."

Palamabron began to yell and to splash violently. "Save me, Theotormon! I can't stay up any longer! I'm too tired! I'll die!"

"Remember what I said about your being alone," Wolff gasped.

Theotormon grinned and dived, and presently he was pushing Palamabron ahead of him. With his head on his brother's buttocks, he pushed, driving with his flippers and his great webbed feet. Palamabron slid from the water and two body length's onto the glassy shore. There he lay, breathing like a sick horse, the water running from his nose and saliva from his mouth.

One by one, Theotormon propelled the others onto the bank, where they lay like dead men. Only Vala refused his offer. She swam as hard as she could, summoning strength that Wolff would not have believed possible she had left. She skidded up a body's length and soon was nudging herself, very slowly, on up the gentle slope. When she had reached a level spot, she carefully got to a sitting position. She looked down at the others and said with scorn, "So these are my brothers? The all-mighty Lords of the universes! A pack of half-drowned rats. Sycophants of a sea-slug, begging for their lives."

Theotormon slid upon the bank and past the men. He walked on his bent legs past Vala and did not look at her. And when the others had regained some of their strength and breath, they too crawled to the level land. They were sorry looking, since most of them had slipped off their clothes and their swords in the water. Only Wolff and Vala had retained their clothes. He had lost all his weapons but his beamer. She still had her sword. Except for her hair, she looked as if she had never been in the water. Her garments had the property of repelling liquids.

Luvah had scooted over to Wolff after trying twice to walk to him and ending on his buttocks both times. His color had come back to his face, so that the freckles across his cheeks and nose did not stand out so sharply. He said, "We were caught by our father as easily as children playing hide-and-seek are caught. Now, from children we have become infants. We cannot even walk, but must crawl like babies. Do you suppose that our father is trying to tell us something?"

"I do not know about that," Wolff said. "But this I do know. Urizen has been planning this for a long

long time. I am beginning to believe that he made the planets that revolve around Appirmatzum for one reason only. This world and the others are designed to torment and to test us."

Luvah laughed without much merriment. "And if we survive the torment and pass the tests, what is our reward?"

"We get a chance to be killed by our father or to kill him."

"Do you really believe he will play fair? Won't he make the stronghold absolutely impregnable? I cannot believe that our father will be fair."

"Fair? What is fair? There is supposed to be an unspoken agreement that every Lord will leave some slight loophole in his defense. Some defect whereby an extremely skillful and clever attacker can get through. Whether this is true in all cases, I do not know. But Lords have been killed or dispossessed, and these Lords thought they were safe from the most powerful and clever. I do not think that the successful ones were successful because of built-in weaknesses by the defender. The chinks in the armor were there for another reason.

"That reason is that the Lords have inherited their weapons. What they haven't inherited or taken from others, they cannot get. The race has lost its ancient wisdom and skill; it has become users, consumers, not creators. So, a Lord must use what he has. And if these weapons do not cover every contingency, if they leave holes in the armor, then they can be penetrated.

"There is another aspect to this. The Lords fight for their lives and fight to kill each other. But most have lived too long. They weary of everything. They want to die. Deep in the abyss of their minds, below the thousands of strata of the years of too much power and too little love, they want to die. And so, there are cracks in the walls."

Luvah was astonished. "You do not really believe this wild theory, brother? I know I am not tired of living. I love life now as much as when I was a hundred. And the others, they fight to live as much as they ever did."

Wolff shrugged and said, "It's only a theory of mine. I have evolved it since I became Robert Wolff. I can see things that I could not see before and that none of you can see."

He crawled to Vala and said, "Lend me your sword for a moment. I want to try an experiment."

"Like cutting my head off?" she said.

"If I wanted to kill you, I have the beamer," he replied.

She took the short blade from its scabbard and handed it to him. He tapped the sharp edge gently on the glassy surface. When the first blow left the stuff unmarked, he struck harder.

Vala said, "What are you doing? You'll ruin the edge."

He pointed at the scratch left by the second blow. "Looks like a scratch made in ice. This stuff is far slipperier, more frictionless than ice, but in other respects it seems to resemble frozen water."

He handed the weapon to her and drew his beamer. After putting it on half-power, he aimed it at a spot on the surface. The stuff grew red, then bubbled. Liquid flowed from it. He turned the beamer off and blew the liquid from the hole. The others crawled over to watch him.

"You're a strange man," Vala said. "Whoever would have thought of doing this?"

"Why is he doing it?" Palamabron said. "Is he crazy, cutting holes in the ground?"

Palamabron had recovered his haughtiness and his

measured way of speaking.

Vala said, "No, he's not crazy. He's curious, that's all. Have you forgotten what it is to be curious, Palamabron? Are you as dead as you look . . . and act. You were certainly lively enough a little while ago."

Palamabron flushed, but he said nothing. He was watching the growth of tiny crystals on the walls of the hole and along the edges of the scratch.

"Self-regeneration," Wolff said. "Now, I have read as much as possible on the old science of our ancestors, but I have never read or heard of anything like this. Urizen must have knowledge lost to others."

"Perhaps," Vala said, "he has gotten it from Red Orc. It is said that Orc knows more than all of the other Lords put together. He is the last of the old ones; it is said that he was born over a half a million years ago."

"It is said. It is said," Wolff mimicked. "The truth is that nobody has seen Red Orc for a hundred millennia. I think he is a dead man but his legend lives on. Enough of this. We have to find the next set of gates, though where those will lead us, I don't know."

He rose carefully and shuffled slowly a few steps forward. The surface of this world was not entirely barren vitreosity. There were widely spaced trees several hundred yards away and between them mushroom-shaped bushes. The trees had thin spiraling trunks that were striped with red and white, like barber poles. The trunks rose straight for twenty feet, then curved to left or right. Where the curve began, branches grew. These were shaped like horizontal 9's and covered with a thin gray fuzz, the strands of which were about two feet long.

Rintrah, naked, shivered and said, "It is not cold,

but something makes me uneasy and quivers through me. Perhaps it is the silence. Listen, and you hear nothing."

They fell silent. There was only a distant soughing, the wind rippling through the bushes and the stiff projections on the end-curled branches, and the slursh-slursh of the river. Aside from that, nothing. No bird calls. No animal cries. No human voices. Only the sound of wind and river and even that hushed as if pressed down by the purple of the skies.

Around them the pale white land rolled away to the four horizons. There were some high rounded hills, the tallest of which was that which had sent them speeding down the hill. From where they stood, they could see its mound and the gate, a tiny dark object, on its top. The rest was low hills and level spaces.

Where do we go from here? Wolff thought. *Without some clue, we could wander forever. We could wander to the end of our lives, provided we find something to eat on the way.*

He spoke aloud. "I believe we should follow along the river. It leads downward, perhaps to some large body of water. Urizen cast us into the river; this may mean that the river is to be our guide to the next gate . . . or gates."

"That may be true," Enion said. "But your father and my uncle has a crooked brain. In his perverse way, he may be using the river as an indication that we should go up it, not down it."

"You may be right, cousin," Wolff replied. "However there is only one way to find out. I suggest we go downriver, if only because it will be easier traveling." He said to Vala, "What do you think?"

She shrugged and said, "I don't know. I picked the wrong gate the last time. Why ask me?"

"Because you were always the closest to father. You know better than the rest of us how he thinks."

She smiled slightly. "I do not think you mean to compliment me by that. But I will take it as such. Much as I hate Urizen, I also admire and respect his abilities. He has survived where most of his contemporaries have not. Since you ask, I say we go downriver."

"How about the rest of you?" Wolff said. He had already made up his mind which direction he was going, but he did not want the others complaining if they went the wrong way. Let them share the responsibility.

Palamabron started to speak. "I say, no, I insist, that . . ."

IX

A WAIL came down against the wind, and they turned to stare upriver. Several hundred yards away, an animal tall as an elephant had appeared from around a hill. Now it stood between two large boulders, the head on the end of its long neck much like that of a camel's with antlers. Its eyes were enormous and its teeth long and sharp, a carnivore's. Its body was red-brown and furry and sloped sharply back from the shoulders. The legs were thin as a giraffe's, despite the heavy body. They ended in great spreading dark-blue cups.

On seeing the cup-feet, Wolff guessed their function. They looked too much like suckers or vacuum pads, which would be one of the few means to enable an animal to walk across this smooth surface.

"Stand still," he said to the others. "We can't run; if we could, there'd be no place to go."

The beast snorted and slowly advanced towards them. It swiveled its neck back and forth, turning its head now and then to look behind it. The right front foot and left rear foot raised in unison, the cups giving a plopping noise. These came down to give it a hold in its forward progress. Then the left front foot and the right rear one raised, and so it came towards them. When it was fifty yards from them, it stopped and raised its head. It gave a cry that was half-bray and half-banshee wail. It lowered its neck until the jaw was on the ground and then scraped the jaw against the ground. The head slid back and forth on the pale surface.

Wolff thought that this motion could be the equivalent of the pawing of dirt of a Terrestrial bull before it charged. He put his beamer on half-power and waited. Suddenly, the creature raised its head as high as it would go, screamed—much like a wounded rabbit—and galloped at them. It was necessarily a slow gallop, since the suction cups did not come off easily. To the humans, it seemed too swift.

Wolff could afford to wait to determine if the beast were bluffing. At twenty yards, he placed the end of the beam at the juncture of neck and chest. Smoke curled up from the red-brown fur, which blackened. The animal screamed again but did not stop its charge. Wolff continued to hold the beam as steadily as he could. Then, seeing that its impetus might carry it to the point where its fanged head could seize them, he switched to full-power.

The beast gave a last scream; its long thin legs crumpled; its body came down on them. The cups stuck to the ground, the legs cracking beneath the weight, the body settling slowly. The neck went limp and the head lolled, the red-purple tongue sticking out, the hazel eyes glassy.

There was silence, broken by Vala's laugh. "There's our dinner and breakfast and dinner again, already cooked for us."

"If it's edible," Wolff said. He watched while Vala and Theotormon, knife handled by one foot, stripped off the hide and cut out half-burnt steaks. Theotormon refused to test the meat. Wolff shuffled forward very carefully, but even so his feet went out from under him. Vala and Theotormon, who had gotten to the beast without slipping, laughed. Wolff arose and continued his journey. He said, "If no one else dares, I'll try the meat. We can't stand around debating whether it's safe or not."

Vala said, "I'm not afraid of it, just disgusted. It has such a rank odor." She bit into it, chewed with distaste, and swallowed. Wolff decided that there was no use his testing it now. With the others, he waited. When a half-hour passed, and Vala showed no ill effects, he started to eat it. The others shuffled or crawled to the carcass and also ate. There was not too much they could stomach, since most of the meat was charred, leaving only a narrow area where the heat had cooked or half-cooked the flesh.

Wolff borrowed Theotormon's knife and cut out other steaks. Reluctantly, because he wished to conserve the power of the beamer, he cooked the steaks. Then they each took an armful and began to march down the river. Wolff lingered for a while, considering the possibility of severing the suction-pads and using them for his locomotion. He gave up the idea after feeling the thickness of the bones of the legs and the toughness of bone and cartilage at juncture of pad and leg. Vala's sword might do the job, but its edge would be too blunted for use afterward.

At the end of a two-mile crawl, they came to a group of bushes near the riverbank. These were three feet high and mushroom in shape, the upper part spreading out far from the slender base. The branches were thick and corkscrew and, like the trees, grew fuzz. At close range, the fuzz looked more like slender needles. There were also large dark-red berries in clusters at the ends of the branches.

Wolff picked one and smelled it. The odor reminded him of pecan nuts. The skin was smooth and slightly moist.

He hesitated about biting into the berry. Again, it was Vala who dared the strange food. She ate one, exclaiming all the while over its deliciousness. A half-hour went by, during which she ate six more. Wolff then ate several. The others picked them off. Palamabron, the last to try them, complained that there were not many left for him.

Vala said, "It is not our fault that you are such a coward."

Palamabron glared at her but did not answer. Theotormon, thinking that here he had found someone who would not dare to answer him back, took up the insults where Vala left off. Palamabron slapped Theotormon in the face. Theotormon bellowed with rage and leaped at Palamabron. His feet slipped out and he skidded on his face into Palamabron's legs. Palamabron went down like a bowling pin. He slid sidewise, out of reach of Theotormon's flailing flipper. Both made a frenzied but vain effort to get at each other's throat.

Finally, Wolff, who had not shared the scornful laughter of the others, called a halt. He said, "If these time-wasting displays of childishness continue, I'll put a stop to them. Not with the beamer, since I don't care to use up power on the likes of you. We'll just go on without you or send you away. We have to have unity and a mimimum of discord. Otherwise, Urizen will have the pleasure of seeing us destroy ourselves."

Theotormon and Palamabron spat at each other but quit their struggles. Silently, in the pale purple shade of the moon overhead, they continued to slide their feet forward. The night had brought an end to the silence. They heard bleatings as of sheep and bellowings as of cattle from a distance. Something roared like a lion. They passed another clump of bushes and saw small bipedal animals feeding off the berries. These were about two and a half feet tall, brown-furred, and lemur-faced. They had big rabbit ears and slit eyes. Their upper legs ended in paws; their lower, in suction discs. They had short scarlet tails, like a rabbit's. On seeing the human beings, they stopped eating and faced them, their noses wiggling. After being convinced that the newcomers were no danger, they resumed eating. But one fellow kept his eyes on them and barked like a dog at them.

Presently, a four-legged animal the size of a Norwegian elkhound came around a low hill. It was shaggy as a sheep-dog, yellowish, and built like a fox. At the ends of its feet were thin skates of bone on which it raced towards the bipeds. These barked in alarm and all took off in a body. They made swift progress, despite the pads, but the skate-wolf was far faster. The leader of the bipeds, seeing that they had no chance, dropped behind until he was even with the slowest of his charges. He shoved against the laggard, knocking him over, then he ran on. The sacrifice screamed and tried to get back up on its suckers, only to be knocked down again by the snarling skate-wolf. There was a brief struggle, ending when the wolf's jaws closed on the biped's throat.

Wolff said, "There's your explanation for the scratches we've seen now and then on the surface. Some of these creatures are skaters."

He was silent for a while, thinking that skates would enable them to make much better progress. The problem was getting them down.

They passed another long-necked, hyena-bodied, deer-antlered beast. This one did not offer to bother them. It bit into a rock of the vitreous substance, ripped out a chunk, and chewed upon it. It kept its eye upon them, groaning with delight at the taste of the rock, its stomach rumbling like defective plumbing in an old house.

They went on and soon came within three hundred yards of a herd of the creatures, all grazing upon the rocks. There were young among them, awkwardly chasing each other in play or nursing from the mothers. Some of the bulls bray-wailed at the intruders, and one kept pace with them for a while. They passed antelope-like animals, marked with red diamond-shapes on white and with two horns that intertwined. Bone skates grew at the end of their legs.

Wolff began to look for a place to sleep. He led them into a semi-amphitheater, a level between four hills. "I'll stand first watch," he said. He designated Luvah as next and Enion after him. Enion protested, asking by what authority Wolff could pick him.

"You can refuse to take your share of responsibility, if you wish," Wolff said. "But if you sleep when your turn comes, you may wake up in the jaws of that."

He pointed past Enion's shoulder, and Enion whirled so swiftly he lost his footing. The others looked in the direction in which Wolff's finger was pointing. On top of one of the hills, a huge maned animal was glaring down at them. Its head was that of a short-snouted crocodile and its body was cat-shaped, the feet ending in broad cups.

Wolff put the beamer on half-power and shot. He flicked the actuation plate briefly and aimed towards the hairs of the mane. The hairs crisped and smoked, and the beast roared, turned, and disappeared beyond the hill.

Wolff said, "Now, somebody has to be officially given authority. So far, we've avoided, that is, you've avoided, a decision. You've more or less let me run things. Mostly because you're too lazy or too occupied with your own petty problems to face this issue. All right, now's the time to settle this. Without a leader whose orders will be immediately obeyed in emergencies, we're all lost. So what do you say?"

"Beloved brother," Vala said, "I think that you have shown that you're the man to follow. I vote for you. Besides, you have the beamer, and that makes you the most powerful of all. Unless, of course, some of us have hidden weapons we've not displayed as yet."

"You're the only one who has enough clothes to conceal weapons," he said. "As for the beamer, whoever is on guard will have it."

They all raised their eyebrows at this. He said, "It's not because I trust your loyalty. It's just that I don't think any of you would be quite stupid enough to try to keep it for yourself or try to take off on your own. When we resume the march, I expect to get the beamer back."

All then voted, except for Palamabron. He said that he did not have to vote, since it was obvious that he would be overruled by the majority, anyway.

"Surely brother, you were not going to nominate yourself," Vala said. "Even you, with all your hideous egotism, could not think of that."

Palamabron ignored her. To Wolff he said, "Why am I not one of the sentinels? Don't you trust me?"

"You can stand first watch tomorrow night," Wolff replied. "Now, let's all get some sleep."

Wolff sat guard while the others slept on their hard beds of white rock. He listened to the distant animal cries: the bray-wails, roars, and some new sounds, a shrill fluting, a plaintive sobbing, a whistling. Once, something beat out a gonging, and there was the flutter of wings overhead. He rose to his feet now and then and slowly pivoted around to cover all points of the compass. At the end of a half-hour, he woke up Enion and gave him the beamer. He had no watch to determine the time, any more than the others did, but, like them, he knew the measured passage of time. As a child, he had gone through a species of hypnosis which enabled him to clock the seconds as accurately as the most precise of chronometers.

For a while, he did not sleep. He was worried

about the first watch of the next night, when Palamabron would be entrusted with the beamer. Of all the Lords, he was the most unstable. He hated Vala even more than the others. Could he withstand the temptation to kill her while she slept? Wolff decided he would have a talk with Palamabron in the morning. His brother must understand that if he killed her, he would have to kill them all. This he could do with the beamer, but he would be alone from then on. This was a curious thing. Though the Lords could not stand to be with each other, they could stand the idea of being alone even less. In other circumstances, they would want no one but themselves, of course. In these, they shared a dread of their father and some comfort in having companions in misery and peril.

Just before he went to sleep, he had an idea. He swore. Why had he not thought of it? Why had not the others? It was so obvious. There was no need to creep and slip along on the ground. With boats, they could travel swiftly and much more surely. They would be safe from the predators. He would see what they could do about this in the morning.

He was propelled from sleep at dawn by shouting. He sat up to see Tharmas shooting at a maned beast, one just like the liongator he had scared off by singeing its hair. The beast came down the hill swiftly, plop-plopping as its suction pads pulled free. Behind it lay three dead mates. The survivor came within ten feet and then dropped, its snout cut half off.

Tharmas held the beamer while he stared at the carcass. Wolff shouted at him to turn the power off. The ray was drilling into the side of the hill. Tharmas suddenly realized what he was doing and deactivated the weapon. By then, most of the charge was gone. Groaning, Wolff took the beamer back. Now he was down to his final power pack.

The others went to work swiftly. They took turns with the knives of Theotormon and Vala and stripped the tough hides off the dead beasts. This was slow work, both because of their ineptness and because they kept sliding on the glassy surface. And they could not refrain from arguing with him, saying that all the hard work was for nothing. Where would he get the framework for the boats he planned? Even if he could use these hides as coverings for the boats, there were not enough to go around.

He told them to shut up and keep on working. He knew what he was doing. With Luvah, Vala, and Theotormon, he shuffled off to the nearest bushes. Here it was necessary to use more power to kill an animal that was eating the berries and refused to give up its claim. It was like a Chinese dragon. It hissed and struck threateningly at them before they got within its range. Its skin was as thick and ridged as armor plate and could be penetrated only by a beam at full-power. Even its eyes were protected. When Wolff shot at these, the ray struck transparent coverings. The creature began waving its head wildly so that Wolff could not keep the beam on one spot. Eventually, he cut through the armor back of the head, and it turned over and died, exposing the serrated plates and tiny suction discs on which it made progress.

"If this keeps up, we'll be out of power," he said to the others. "Pray that that time does not come."

Wolff tested the toughness of the bark of the bushes and found it to be strong indeed. Chopping down the bushes and slicing off lengths to make a framework for the rough coracles he had in mind would be long hard work and ruin the sword. It was then, glancing at the caterdragon—as he called it— that he saw a ready-made vessel. Well, not quite finished, but it should need less work to complete than the original boat he had in mind.

The sword, driven by his powerful arm, was equal to the task of separating the caterdragon's locomotion plates from the body armor. Thereafter, the sword and the knife cut up the internal organs. By then the other Lords were with them, and they took turns at the work. All were soon covered with blood, which also ran over the area and made the surface eves more frictionless. Several of the liongators, attracted by the odor of blood, and then driven frantic by it, attacked. Wolff had to expend more power in killing them.

The only possible sources for paddles were the 9-shaped branches on the trees. The bark of these resisted the edge of the sword. Again, Wolff had to use his beamer. He cut enough branches to make ten paddles, three extra, since Theotormon could not handle one with his flippers. The needles came off easily when cut with a knife.

They had a rather flexible canoe, sixty feet long. The only openings to worry about were the mouth and nostrils. These were disposed of by bending the hollow front part back and up and tying a small boulder to it with Vala's cloak. The weight of the boulder stopped the forward part from straightening out and thus kept it above the water level—they hoped. Again, Wolff had to use some more power to burn off the pieces of gristle and the blood that adhered to the inside walls of the armor-plate. Then, walking on their knees, the Lords shoved their makeshift boat towards the river.

Near the edge of the river, they rose to their feet and got into the dragonboat by falling over the sides and into the bottom. They did so by teams of twos, one on each side, to keep the craft from falling to one side. When all but Wolff and Vala had gotten in, the two urged the boat down. Fortunately, there was a very gentle incline. As the craft picked up a little speed, Wolff and Vala clung to the sides and the others pulled them aboard.

The night-bringing moon crossed the horizon, and the dragoncraft floated with the current. Two Lords stayed on paddle-duty to keep the boat straight while the others tried to sleep. The moon passed, and after it came the bright purple of the naked skies. The river was smooth, disturbed only by tiny waves and ripples. They passed through canyons and came out again between rolling ground. The day passed without incident. They complained about the stench from the meat and blood they had not been able to clear away. They made jokes as each had to rid himself of food and drink. They spoke grouchily of their lack of sleep the previous night. They talked about what might face them when—or if—they ever found the gate that would lead them into the palace of their father.

A day and a night floated by. Several hours after the second dawn, they came around a wide bend of the river. Ahead was a rock that split the river, a dome of white about thirty feet high. On top of it, side by side, was a pair of towering and golden hexagonal frames.

X

FROM THE EDGE of the river, where the dragonboat
was beached, Wolff studied the problem. It was useless to try to climb the near-perpendicular and near-
frictionless rock without some aids. A rope had to be
thrown up to catch on something. The hexagons
were too wide to try to settle a noose around them.

A grappling hook might do the job. It could be
presumed that the other side of the gate—that which
opened onto another planet, he hoped—would hold a
grapple.

The hides of animals could be cut and tied or sewn
together to make a rope, although the strips would
have to be tanned to give them flexibility. The metal
for the hooks was a big problem.

There might be metal somewhere in this world,
perhaps not too far away. But getting to it across the
land would be a slow process. So, there was only one
thing to do, and he did not expect that the two most
vital in this particular project would be cooperative.

Nor were they. Vala did not want to give up her
sword and Theotormon refused to part with his knife.

Wolff argued with them for several hours, pointing
out that if they did not give up their weapons, they
would be dead in time anyway.

Wolff said, after Theotormon's violent refusal,
"Very well. Be pig-headed. But if the rest of us find a
way to get through the gate, we will not take you with
us. I swear it! You will be pushed back into this pale
world of icestone, and you will stay here until an
animal devours you or you die of old age."

Vala looked around at the Lords who sat in a circle
about her. She smiled and said, "Very well. You may
have my sword."

("You won't get my knife, I promise you that," Theotormon said.

The others began to scoot on their buttocks towards him. He stood up and tried to run past them. His huge feet gave him a better grip on the white stuff than the others could manage, but Wolff reached out and clutched his ankle, and he went down. He fought as best he could, submerged under the pile of bodies. Eventually, weeping, he gave up. Then, muttering, scowling, he went off to sit down on the river's edge by himself.

With some chalky stone he found, Wolff traced lines on Vala's sword. He set the beamer at full power and quickly cut out triangles. He then arranged the three pieces and set several round pieces of the sword on top of them. With the beamer at half-power he fused the three prongs and round pieces into a single unit. After plunging these into cold water, he heated the prongs in their middles and hammered them into slightly hooked shapes. He curved another strip of sword with heat and hammered and fused this onto the top of the prong so that a rope could be tied around it.

Since he did not have to use Theotormon's knife, he gave it back to him. He cut the end of Vala's sword into a point and thus provided her with a somewhat short sword. As he pointed out, it was better than nothing.

Making the rope took several days. It was not difficult to kill and flay the animals and then cut out strips for rope lengths. Tanning presented difficulties. He searched for materials but could find nothing. Finally, he decided to grease the plaited rawhide with animal fat and hope for the best.

One dawn, as the empurpling shadow of the moon withdrew, the dragonboat was launched well above the gaterock. With the Lords behind him paddling backwards, Wolff stood up in the prow, and he cast the grapple upwards in an arc and released the rope after it.

The three-pronged device went through the gate and disappeared. He pulled in on it as the boat rammed into the base of the rock. For a second, he thought he had a hold. Then the grapple came flying out of the gate, and he fell back. He caught himself, but the uneasy equilibrium of the boat was upset. It turned over, and all went into the water. They clung to the upturned bottom, and Wolff managed to keep hold of the rope and grapple.

A half-hour later, they tried again.

"Try and try again," Wolff told them. "That's an old Earth saying."

"Spare me your proverbs," Rintrah said. "I'm soaked as a drowning rat and as miserable. Do you think there's any use trying again?"

"What else is there to do? Let's get at it. Give it the old college try."

They looked at him uncomprehendingly and then reluctantly launched the boat again. Now Wolff made a more difficult cast. He threw for the very top of the hexagon. It was at least twelve feet high, which made the top of the frame forty-two feet above water. Nevertheless, he threw well, the prongs gripping the other side of the frame.

"I got it!" he said grinning. He pulled in on the rope to take up the slack. The boat slid on by the right side of the rock, rubbing against it. He ordered the men to continue backwatering, which they tried without success. The boat began to bend as the current wrapped it around the rock. Wolff, in the bow, knew that if he continued to be carried with the boat, he would slide the prongs sidewise off the top of the frame.

He clung to the rawhide rope and allowed the boat

to be taken off from under him. Then Wolff was hanging onto the rope, his feet in the water. He lifted his feet to brace himself against the rock, only to have them slide away. He quit this method of climbing and hauled himself up, hand-over-hand, on the greasy rope. This was not easy to do, since the rock curved just gently enough to make the rope follow it closely, the tension being greatest just above his handhold. Without slack, he had to force his hands to slide between rope and rock.

He rose slowly. Halfway up, he felt the tension go. There was a crack, barely audible above the swirl of water at the rock-base. Yelling with disappointment, he fell back into the river.

When he was hauled out by Vala and Enion, he discovered that two of the prongs had broken across where they joined the top part. The pieces were now somewhere at the bottom of the river.

"What do we do now?" Palamabron snarled at him. "You have used up all our weapons and drained your beamer of much of its power. And we are no closer to getting through the gate than before. Less, I say. Look at us. Look at me. Spouting water like an old fish brought up from the abyss and weary, oh, Los, how weary!"

"Go fly a kite," Wolff said. "Another old Earth saying."

He stopped, eyes widening, and said, "I wonder . . ."

Palamabron threw his hands up into the air and said, "Oh, no, not another of your wonderful ideas!"

"Wonderful or not, they're ideas," Wolff said. "So far, I'm the only one who's had anything to offer . . . besides whinings, complaints, and backbitings."

He lay on his back for a while, staring up at the purple skies and chewing on a piece of meat Luvah had handed him. Was a kite a fantastic thought? Even if it could be built, would it work?

He discarded the kite. If one were made big enough to carry a heavy prong, it would not go through the hexagon. Wait a minute. What if the kite, dangling a hook on the end of a rope, were flown above the hexagon? He groaned and gave up the kite again. It just would not work.

Suddenly, he sat up and shouted. "It might do it! Two!"

"Two what?" Luvah said, startled out of his drowse.

"Not kites!"

"Who said anything about kites?" Luvah replied.

"Two boats and two good men to throw," Wolff cried. "It might work. It better. I've about exhausted my ideas, and it's evident I'm not going to get any from the rest of you. You've used your brains these many thousands of years for only one purpose: to kill each other. You're good for nothing else. But, by Los, I'm going to make you good for something else!"

"You're tired," Vala said. "Lie down and rest." She was grinning at him. That surprised him. Now, what would she be amused about? She was wet and muscle-aching and as frustrated as the others.

Could it be that she still had some love for him beneath that hate? Perhaps she was proud of him that he continued to improvise and to fight while the others only nursed their resentments.

Or was she trying to make him think that she still loved him and was proud of him? Did she have a secret reason for this display of amiability?

He did not know. To be a Lord was to mistrust every motive of another Lord, and with good reason.

By the time the first two coracles were half-made, Wolff changed his plan. Originally, he had wanted to have two of the little round boats approach the gate-rock on each side. But then he decided that three would be better.

Using wood of the bushes and tree branches and strips of hide for ties, he made a high scaffolding. Each of its four legs was placed on a boat, one on the dragoncraft and each one of the other three on a coracle. Then, after rehearsing the Lords many times in what they must do, Wolff began the operation. Slowly, the boats at the base of the rectangular scaffolding were pushed into the water. The current near the shore was not as swift as out in the river's center, so the Lords could keep it from being carried off at once. While they swam and shoved against the boats, Wolff climbed up the narrow ladder built on one leg of the scaffolding. This was supported by the larger dragon boats, and thus the leg with Wolff on it did not tip over too far. Even so, for a moment, he feared a turnover. Then, as he hitched himself on his belly along the planking of the scaffolding, the structure righted.

The other Lords, working in teams, climbed into the big boat and the three small ones. They went in simultaneously, to distribute the weight equally. Vala, Theotormon, and Luvah were each already in a coracle, and they helped Palamabron, Enion, and Ariston. Tharmas was very agile; he got into the dragonboat with a quick heave and twist of his body.

The Lords began paddling to direct the scaffolding. They had some trouble at first, since the coracles, built more like tubs than boats, were difficult to navigate. But they had launched the structure well above their goal so that they could get the feel of their awkward craft before they reached the rock. Wolff clung to the forward part of the structure, the bridge, which projected out above the water. The bridge pitched and rolled, and twice he thought sure that it would go over with him. Then the white dome of the rock with the twin golden hexagons was dead ahead. He shouted down to the Lords, and they began backpaddling. It was vital that the scaffolding not crash into the rock with much speed. Fragile, it could not resist a strong impact.

Wolff had decided that he would enter the left gate, since the last time they had taken the right. But as the end of the bridge neared, the scaffolding veered. The bridge drove in at a slant towards the left hexagon. Wolff rose to a crouch, and, as the structure rammed with a loud noise into the rock, he leaped forward. He shot through the hexagon with his beamer in his belt and a rope coiled around his shoulders.

XI

HE DID NOT HAVE the slightest idea of what he would find on the other side. He expected either another planet or Urizen's stronghold. He suspected that Urizen was not through playing with them, and that he would find himself on the third of the planets that revolved around Appirmatzum. He might have a comfortable landing or be dropping into a pit of wild beasts or down a precipice.

As he landed, he realized that he had come in against an incline. He bent his knees and put out his hands and so stopped himself from banging into the stone. It was smooth but not frictionless, and it leaned away from him at a forty-five degree angle. Turning, he saw why the grapples had slid back out of the gate at his first experiment. The base of the hexagon on this side was set flush with the stone. There was no purchase for any hold.

He smiled, knowing that his father had foreseen hooks and had set up the trap against them. But his son had gotten through.

Wolff pushed against the seemingly empty area within the hexagon. Unlike the gate through which they had entered the waterworld, this was not one-way. Urizen did not care, for some reason or another, whether they went back into the planet of purple skies. Or he knew that they would never want to return to it.

Wolff climbed up the stone incline, which was set on the side of a hill. He tied one end of his rope around a small tree and then went back to the gate. He flipped the free end of the rope through the gate. It jerked, and presently Vala's face appeared. He helped her through, and the two of them grabbed hold of the other Lords as they climbed through.

When Rintrah, the last, was safe, Wolff stuck his head through the gate for a final look. He made it quick, because it gave him a frightening feeling to know that his body was on a planet twenty thousand miles distant from his head. And it would be a grim joke, exactly to his father's tastes, if Urizen should deactivate the gate at that moment.

The end of the bridge was only three feet from the hexagon. The scaffolding was still holding straight, although in time the currents would swing one of the boats supporting a leg and carry off the whole structure.

He withdrew his head, his neck feeling as if it had just escaped a guillotine.

The Lords should have been exultant, but they were too tired from their labors, and they were burdened with the future. By now, they knew that they were on another of the satellites of Appirmatzum. The sky was a deep yellow. The land around them was, apart from this hill, flat. The ground was covered with a six-inch high grass, and there were many bushes. These were much like the Terrestrial plants Wolff knew. There were at least a dozen species which bore berries of different sizes, colors, and shapes.

The berries had one thing in common, however. They all had a very disagreeable odor.

Near the hill of the gate was the shore of a sea. Along the sea ran a broad yellow sandbeach that extended as far as they could see. Wolff looked inland and saw mountains. The side of one had some curious formations that resembled a face. The longer he looked at it, the more sure he was that it was a face.

He said to the other Lords, "Our father has given us a sign, I think. A marker on the road to the next gate. I also think that he is not directing us just for our benefit.''

They started across the plain towards the distant ranges. Presently, they came to a broad river and followed its course. They found its water to be pure and sweet, and they ate the meat and berries they had brought with them from the white-and-purple world. Then the night-bringing moon swung around the horizon. This was mauve and, like the other satellites, swept the surface of the primary with a pale dusk.

They slept and marched all the next day. They were a silent troop now, tired and footsore and nervous because of their lack of weapons. Their silence was also a reflection of the hush of this world. Not an animal or bird cried, nor did they see any life besides themselves and the vegetation. Several times they thought they saw a small creature in the distance, but when they neared the place, they could find nothing.

The mountains were three days away. As they got closer, the features became more distinct. The evening of the second day, the face became that of Urizen. It was smiling at them, the eyes looking down. Then the Lords became even more silent and startful, since they could not escape the gigantic stone face of their father. Always, he seemed to be mocking them.

Halfway through the fourth day, they stood at the foot of the mountain and below the brobdingnagian chin of Urizen. The mountain was of solid stone, flesh-pink and very hard. Near where they stood was an opening, a narrow canyon that rose to the top of the mountain, at least ten thousand feet above.

Wolff said, ''There doesn't seem any other way to go than through there. Unless we go around the mountains. And I think we'd be wasting our time if we did that.''

Palamabron said, "Why should we do what our father wants?"

"We have no choice," Wolff said.

"Yes, we'll dance to his tune, and then he'll catch us and spit us on a roast, like fowl," Palamabron said. "I have a notion to quit this trudging, this weary weary road."

"And where will you settle down?" Vala said. "Here? In this paradise? You may be too stupid to have noticed it, brother, but we are almost out of food. The meat is almost gone, and we ate the last of the berries this morning. We have seen nothing on this world that seems edible. You may try the berries, if you wish. But I think they're poisonous."

"Oh, Los! Do you think Urizen means to starve us to death?" Palamabron said.

Wolff said, "I think we'll starve unless we find some food. And we won't find any standing here."

He led the way into the canyon. Their path took them on smooth bare rock that had once been the bed of the stream. The river had shifted to the other side of the canyon and was now several feet below the stone banks. Bushes grew sparsely on the lip of the stone.

The Lords followed a meandering course all day. That night, they ate the last of their food. When dawn came, they rose with empty bellies and a feeling that this time their fortune had deserted them. Wolff led them as swiftly as he dared, thinking that the sooner they got out of the gloomy canyon, the better. Moreover, this place offered no food. There were no fish in the river; there were not even insects.

The second day of their starvation, they saw their first living creature. They came around a bend, all silent and walking slowly. Their noiselessness, plus their approach from downwind, enabled them to be close to the animal before it detected them. Two feet high, it was standing on its kangaroo-like hind legs and holding a branch with two lemur-like front paws. On seeing them, it quit eating the berries, glanced wildly around, and then launched itself away with great leaps. Its long thin tail projected stiffly behind it.

Wolff started to run after it, but quit as soon as he realized its speed. The animal stopped when it was a hundred yards away and turned to face them. Its head was much like a purebred Persian cat's except that the ears were a jackrabbit's. The body was khaki; the head, chocolate; the ears, magenta.

Wolff advanced steadily towards it, and it fled until it was out of sight. He decided that it would be a good thing if the Lords had clubs in case they came within close range of the hopper again. He cut the bushes to make sticks that would be heavy enough to do the job.

Palamabron asked him why he did not kill the beast with his beamer. Wolff answered that he was trying to waste as little power as possible. The thing took off so swiftly that he was not sure he could hit it. The next time, power conservation or not, he would shoot. They had to have something to eat. They continued on their way and began seeing more of the hoppers. These must have been warned by the first, since they all kept well out of range.

Two hours later, they came to a wide fissure in the canyon walls. Wolff went down it and found that it led to a box canyon. This was about thirty feet lower than the main one, about three hundred yards wide and four hundred deep. The floor was thick with bushes, among which he saw one hopper.

He went back to the others and told them what they were to do. Luvah and Theotormon stayed within the narrow passage while the rest walked out into the canyon. They spread out in a wide circle to close in on the lone animal.

The hopper stood in a large clearing, its nose twitching, its head turning quickly from side to side. Wolff told the others to stop, and he walked slowly towards it, the club held behind his back. The animal waited until Wolff was within ten feet of it. Then it disappeared.

Wolff whirled around, thinking that it had jumped with such swiftness that he had not been able to see it. There was no animal behind him. There were only the Lords, gaping and asking what had happened.

Approximately three seconds later, the beast reappeared. It was now thirty feet from him. Wolff took a step towards it, and it was gone again.

Three seconds later, there were two animals in the clearing. One was ten feet away from Vala. The other was to Wolff's left and fifteen feet away.

"What the hell?" Wolff said. It took much to startle him. Now he was far more than startled. He was bewildered.

The animal near Vala disappeared. Now there was one left. Wolff ran towards it, his club raised and shouting, hoping to freeze the animal long enough to get a chance to strike it.

It vanished. A little later, it reappeared to his right. A second hopper was with it.

The Lords closed in on them. The two beasts suddenly became five.

After that, there was much yelling, screaming, and confusion. Some of the animals had popped up behind the Lords, and several Lords turned to give chase.

Then there were two of the creatures that Wolff was to call tempusfudgers.

These two became three as the wild chase continued for another three seconds.

Then there was one.

The Lords pursued that one and suddenly had two before them.

Three animals were being chased three seconds later.

Then there was one.

The Lords came in on it from all directions at full speed. Two animals reappeared, one directly in front of Palamabron. He was so startled, he tried to stop, stumbled, and fell on his face. The creature hopped over him and then vanished as Rintrah swung at it with his stick.

There were two now.

Three.

All of a sudden, none.

The Lords stopped running and stared at each other. Only the wind and their heavy breathing sounded in the box canyon.

Abruptly three of the beasts were in their midst.

The chase started again.

There was one.

Five.

Three.

Six.

For six seconds, three.

Six again.

Wolff called a halt to the milling chase. He led the Lords back to the entrance, where they sat down to recover their breath. Having done that, they began chattering away to each other, all asking the same questions and no one with an answer.

Wolff studied the six animals a hundred yards away. They had forgotten their panic, though not the cause of it, and were nibbling away at the berries.

A silence fell upon the Lords again. They looked at their pensive brother, and Vala said, "What do you make of it, Jadawin?"

"I've been thinking back to the time that the first

animal we saw vanished," he said. "I've been trying to calculate the lengths of their disappearances and the correlation between the number at one time and at succeeding times."

He shook his head. "I don't know. Maybe. It doesn't seem possible. But how else explain it. Or, if not explain, describe, anyway.

"Tell me, have any of you ever heard of a Lord having success with time-travel experiments?"

Palamabron laughed.

Vala said, "Jackass!" She spoke to Wolff. "I have heard that Blind Orc tried for many years to discover the principles of time. But it is said that he gave up. He claimed that trying to dissect time was a problem as insolvable as explaining the origin of the universe."

"Why do you ask?" Ariston said.

"There is a tiny subatomic particle which Earth scientists call the neutrino," Wolff answered. "It's an uncharged particle with zero rest mass. Do you know what I'm talking about?"

All shook their heads. Luvah said, "You know we were all exceedingly well educated at one time, Jadawin. But it has been thousands of years since we took any interest in science except to use the devices we had at hand for our purposes."

"You are indeed a bunch of ignorant gods," Wolff said. "The most powerful beings of the cosmos, yet barbaric, illiterate divinities."

"What has that got to do with our present situation?" Enion said. "And why do you insult us? You yourself said we must quit these insults if we are to survive."

"Forgive me," Wolff said. "It's just that I am sometimes overwhelmed at the discrepancy . . . never mind. Anyway, the neutrino behaves rather peculiarly. In such a manner, in fact, that it might be said to go backward in time."

"It really does?" Palamabron said.

"I doubt it. But it's behavior can be described in time-travel terms, whether the neutrino actually does go into reverse chronological gear or not.

"I believe the same applies to those beasts out there. Maybe they can go forward or backwards in time. Perhaps Urizen had the power to create such animals. I doubt it. He may have found them in some universe we don't know about and imported them.

"Whatever their origin, they do have an ability which makes them *seem* to hop around in time. Within a three-second limit, I'd say."

He drew a circle in the dirt with the end of his stick. "This represents the single animal we first saw."

He drew a line from it and described another circle at its end. "This represents the disappearance of it, its nonexistence in our time. It was going forward in time, or seemed to."

"I'll swear it was not gone for three seconds when it first disappeared," Vala said.

Wolff extended a line from the second circle and made a third circle at its end. Then he scratched a line at right angles to it, and bent it back to a position opposite the second circle.

"It leaped forward into time, or can be described as doing so. Then it went back to the time-slot it did not occupy when it made the first jump. Thus, we saw a beast for six seconds but did not know that it had gone forward and backward.

"Then the animal—let's call it a tempusfudger— jumped forward again to the time at which its first— avatar—had come out of the first jump.

"Now we have two. The same animal, fissioned by time-travel.

"One jumped the three seconds forward again, and we did not see it during that time. The other did not jump but ran about. It jumped when tempus-fudger No. 2 reappeared.

"Only No. 1 also jumped back just as No. 2 came out of the time-hop. So we have two again."

"But all of a sudden there were five?" Rintrah said.

"Let's see. We had two. Now No. 1 had made a jump, and he was one of the five. He jumped back to be one of the previous two. Then he jumped forward again to become No. 3 of the five.

"No. 2 had jumped, when there was only one tempusfudger, to become No. 2 of the five. No. 1 and No. 2 jumped forward and then back to also become No. 4 and 5 of the five.

"No. 4 and 5 then jumped ahead to the period when there were only two. Meanwhile, No. 1 had leaped over three seconds, No. 4 didn't leap, and No. 5 did. So there were only two at that instant."

He grinned at their lax faces. "Now do you understand?"

"That's impossible," Tharmas said. "Time-travel! You know it's impossible!"

"Sure, I know. But if these animals aren't time-traveling, what are they doing? You don't know any more than I do. So, if I can describe their behavior as chronosaltation, and the description helps us catch them, why object?"

"Why don't you use your beamer?" Rintrah said. "We're all very hungry. I'm weak after chasing those flickering on-again-off-again things."

Wolff shrugged and arose and walked towards the fudgers. They continued eating but kept watching him. When he was within thirty yards, they hopped away. He followed them until they were getting close to the blind wall of the canyon. They scattered. He put the beamer on half-power and aimed at one.

Perhaps the tempusfudger was startled by the raising of the weapon. It disappeared just as he fired, and the beam's energy was absorbed by a boulder beyond it.

He cursed, flicked off the power, and aimed at another. This leaped to one side and avoided the first shot. He kept the power on and swung the beam to catch it. The animal jumped again, narrowly escaping the ray. Wolff twisted his wrist to bring the fudger within touch of the beam. The animal disappeared.

Quickly, he swung the weapon back towards the others. A fudger sprang across his field of vision, and he brought the white ray upon it.

It disappeared at the same time. There was a shout behind him. He turned to see the Lords pointing at a dead animal a few yards to his left. It lay in a heap, its fur scorched.

He blinked. Vala came running and said, "It dropped out of the air; it was dead and cooked when it hit the ground."

"But I didn't hit anything except just now," he said. "And the animal I hit hasn't reappeared yet."

"That fudger was dead on arrival three seconds ago, maybe a little more," she said. "Three seconds before you hit the other."

She stopped, grinned, and said, "What do I mean . . . other? It's the same one you hit. Killed before you hit it. Or just as you hit it. Only it jumped back."

Wolff said, slowly, "You're telling me I killed it first, then shot it."

"No, not really. But it looked that way. Oh, I don't know. I'm confused."

"Anyway, we have something to eat," he said. "But not much. There's not enough meat there to satisfy us."

He whirled and brought the beam around to describe a horizontal arc. It struck some rocks, then came to a fudger. And the beam went out.

He continued to aim the beamer steadily at the fudger, which stood poised upon its hind legs, its big eyes blinking.

"The power's gone," he said. He ejected the power pack and stuck the beamer into his belt. It was useless now, but he had no intention of throwing it away. The time might come when he would get his hands on some fresh packs.

He wanted to continue the hunt with sticks. The others vetoed him. Weak and hungry, they needed food at once. Although the meat was half-charred, they devoured it greedily. Their bellies quit rumbling a little. They rested a moment, then got to their feet and went after the tempusfudgers again.

Their plan was to spread out in a wide circle which would contract to bring all the animals within reach of the clubs. The fudgers began hopping wildly and flickering in and out of existence . . . or time. At one moment, there were none, when all must have simultaneously decided to jump forward or to jump backward. It was difficult to tell what was going on during the hunt.

Wolff made no effort at the beginning to keep count. There were six, then zero, and then six, then three, then six, then one, then seven.

Back and forth, in and out, while the Lords ran around and howled like wolves and swung their sticks, hoping to connect with a fudger just as it came out of the chronoleap. Suddenly, Tharmas' club thudded against the side of the head of one of the animals as it materialized. It collapsed, jerked several times, and died.

Eight had dropped out of the air. One had stayed behind as a carcass while the others became invisible. There should have been seven the next time, but there were eight again. Three seconds later, there were three. Another three seconds, nine. Zero. Nine. Two. Eleven. Seven. Two.

Eleven, and Wolff threw his stick and caught one in the back. It pitched forward on its face. Vala was on it with her stick and beat it to death before it could recover from its stunned condition.

There were fifteen, quickly cut to thirteen when Rintrah and Theotormon each killed one. Then, zero.

Within a minute, the tempusfudgers seemed to go riot. Terrified, they hurled themselves back and forth and became twenty-eight, zero, twenty-eight, zero, and fifty-six, or so Wolff roughly estimated it. It was, of course, impossible to make an accurate count. A little later, he was sure, only because his arithmetic assured him it should be so, that the doubling had resulted in one thousand seven hundred and ninety-two.

There had been no more casualties among the fudgers to reduce the number. The Lords had been unable to kill any. They were being buffeted by the ever-increasing horde, knocked down by hoppers appearing in front of them, behind them, and beside them, stepped upon, scratched, kicked, and hammered.

Suddenly, the little animals stampeded towards the exit of the canyon. They hurtled over the floor and should have jammed into the narrow pass, but somehow formed an orderly arrangement and were gone.

Slowly, sore and shaken, the Lords arose. They looked at the four dead animals and shook their heads. Out of almost eighteen hundred that had been at hand, easy prey—in theory—these pitiful four were left.

"Half a fudger will make one good meal for each of

us," Vala said. "That's better than none. But what will we do tomorrow?"

The others did not answer. They began collecting wood for the cooking fires. Wolff borrowed Theotormon's knife and started the skinning.

In the morning, they ate the scraps left over from the evening's feast. Wolff led them on up. The canyon remained as silent as before, except for the river's murmuring. The walls kept on pressing in. The sky burned yellow far above. Fudgers appeared at a distance. Wolff tried throwing rocks at them. He almost struck one, only to see it disappear as if it had slipped around a corner of air. It came into sight again, three seconds later, twenty feet away and hopping as if it had an important engagement it had suddenly recalled.

Two days after they had last eaten, the Lords were almost ready to try the berries. Palamabron argued that the repulsive odor of the berries did not necessarily mean that they had a disagreeable taste. Even if they did, they were not necessarily poisonous. They were going to die, anyway, so why not test the berries?

"Go ahead," Vala said. "It's your theory and your desire. Eat some!"

She was smiling peculiarly at him, as if she were enjoying the conflict between his hunger and fear.

"No," Palamabron said. "I will not be your guinea pig. Why should I sacrifice myself for all of you? I will eat the berries only if all eat at the same time."

"So you can die in good company," Wolff said. "Come on, Palamabron. Put up or shut up—old Earth proverb. You're wasting our time arguing. Either do it yourself or forget about it."

Palamabron sniffed at the berry he was holding, made a face, and let the berry fall on the rocky floor.

Wolff started to walk away, and the Lords followed. About an hour later, he saw another side-canyon. On the way into it, he picked up a round stone which was just the right size and weight for throwing. If only he could sneak up close enough to a fudger and throw the rock while it was looking the other way.

The canyon was a little smaller than that in which the Lords had made their first hunt. At its far end was a single tempusfudger, eating the berries. Wolff got down on his hands and knees and began the slow crawl towards it. He took advantage of every rock for covering and managed to get halfway across the canyon before the animal noticed anything. It suddenly quit moving its jaws, sat up, and looked around, its nose wiggling, its ears vibrating like a TV antenna in a strong wind.

Wolff hugged the ground and did not move at all. He was sweating with the effort and tension, since the starvation diet had weakened him considerably. He wanted to jump up and run at the fudger and hurl himself upon it, tear it apart, eat it raw. He could have devoured the entire animal from the tips of its ears down to the tip of its tail and then broken the bones open to suck out the marrow.

He forced himself to stay motionless. The animal must get over its suspiciousness soon, after which Wolff could resume his turtle-like approach.

Then, from behind a rock near the fudger, another beast appeared. It was gray except for red wolflike ears, had a long pointed face, a bushy tail, and was about midway in size between a fox and a coyote. It sprang at the tempusfudger, coming up from behind it just as it was looking the other way.

Its teeth closed on air. The fudger had disappeared, escaping the jaws by a fraction of an inch.

The predator also disappeared, vanishing before it struck the ground.

Three animals appeared, two fudgers and one predator. Wolff, who liked to tag unknown things, at once called it a chronowolf. For the first time, he was seeing the creature that nature—or Urizen—had placed here to keep the fudger from overpopulating this world.

Wolff now had time to figure out what was happening with the leapers. There had been two. Then there were none. Then, three. So the original fudger and the chronowolf had jumped ahead. But the fudger had stayed only a microsecond, and leaped back also. So that he had reproduced himself and now there were two for the wolf to chase.

Again, the animals vanished. They reappeared, four in number. Two fudgers, two chronowolves. The chase was on, not only in space but in the strange gray corridors of backwards-forwards time.

Another simultaneous jump into the tempolimbo. Wolff ran towards a boulder around which grew a number of bushes. He hurled himself down and then peered between the bushes.

Seven again. This time a wolf had come out of wherever he had been just behind his quarry. He hurled himself forward, and his jaws closed around the neck of the fudger. There was a loud crack; the fudger dropped dead.

Seven living, and one dead. A fudger had gone back and then forward again.

The living vanished. Evidently the wolf did not intend to stay behind and eat his kill.

Then six were jumping around the plain. Savagely, a wolf bit another wolf on the neck, and the attacked crumpled in death.

Nothing for three seconds. Wolff ran out and threw himself down on the ground. Although not hidden behind anything this time, he hoped that his motionlessness, combined with the terror of the fudgers and the bloodlust of the wolves, would make them not notice him.

Another wolf had been born out of time's womb. Parthenogenesis of chronoviators.

Two wolves launched themselves at each other, while the third watched them, and the fudgers hopped around in apparent confusion.

The observer predator became participant, not in the struggle between his fellows, but in the hunt. He caught a fudger by the throat as it hurtled by him in its blind panic.

A fudger and a wolf died.

The living flickered out again. When they came back into his sight, a wolf gripped a fudger's neck and cracked it.

Wolff slowly rose to his feet. At the exact moment that one of the wolves died, he hurled his stone at the winner. It must have caught the motion out of the corner of its eyes, since it vanished just before the stone would have struck. And when it shot out of the chute of time, it was going as swiftly as its four legs would take it towards the exit.

"I'm sorry to deprive you of the spoils of victory," Wolff called out after it. "But you can resume the hunt eleswhere."

He went to call the other Lords and to tell them that their luck had changed. Six animals would fill their bellies and furnish a little over for the next day.

There came the time again when the Lords had been without food for three days. They were gaunt, their cheeks hollow, their eyes crouched within dark and deep caves, their bellies advancing towards their spines. That day Wolff sent them out in pairs to hunt. He had intended to go alone but Vala insisted that he take Luvah with him. She would hunt by herself. Wolff asked her why she wanted it that way, and she replied that she did not care to be accompanied by only one man.

"You think you might become the victim of a cannibal?" Wolff said.

"Exactly," she said. "You know that if we continue to go hungry, it's inevitable that we'll start eating one another. It may even have been planned by Urizen. He would very much enjoy seeing us kill one another and stuff our bellies with our own flesh and blood."

"Have it your own way," Wolff said. He left with Luvah to explore a series of side-canyons. The two sighted a number of fudgers eating from bushes and began the patient, hours-long creeping upon them. They came within an inch of success. The stone, thrown by Wolff, went past the head of his intended victim. After that, all was lost. The fudgers did not even bother to take refuge in time but leaped away and were lost in another canyon.

Wolff and Luvah continued to look until near the time for the moon to bring another night of hunger-torn sleeplessness. When they got back to the meeting-place, they found the others, looking very perturbed. Palamabron and his hunting-companion, Enion, were missing.

"I don't know about the rest of you," Tharmas said, "but I'm too exhausted to go looking for the damn fools."

"Maybe we should," Vala said. "They might have had some luck and even now be stuffing themselves with good meat, instead of sharing it with us."

Tharmas cursed. However, he refused to search for them. If they had had luck, he said, he would know it when he next saw their faces. They would not be able to hide their satisfaction from him. And he would kill them for their selfishness and greed.

"They wouldn't be doing anything you wouldn't if you had their chance," Wolff said. "What's all the uproar about? We don't know that they've caught anything. After all, it was only a suggestion by Vala. There's no proof, not the slightest."

They grumbled and cursed but soon were alseep with utter weariness.

Wolff slept, too, but awoke in the middle of the night. He thought he had heard a cry in the distance. He sat up and looked at the others. They were all there, except for Palamabron and Enion.

Vala sat up also. She said, "Did you hear something, brother? Or was it the wailing of our bellies?"

"It came from upriver," he said. He rose to his feet. "I think I shall go look."

She said, "I'll go with you. I cannot sleep any longer. The thought that they might be feasting keeps me angry and awake."

"I do not think the feasting will be on the little hoppers," he said.

She said, "You think . . ."

"I do not know. You spoke of the possibility. It becomes stronger every day, as we become weaker and hungrier."

He picked up his stick, and they walked along the edge of the river. They had little difficulty seeing where they were going. The moon brought only a half-darkness. Even though the walls of the canyon deepened the twilight, there was still enough light for them to proceed with confidence.

So it was that they saw Palamabron before he saw them. His head appeared for a moment above a boulder near the wall of the canyon. His profile was presented to them, then he disappeared. On bare feet, they crept towards him. The wind carried to them the noise he was making. It sounded as if he were striking one stone against another.

"Is he trying to make a fire?" Vala whispered.

Wolff did not answer. He was sick, since he could think of only one reason why Palamabron would want to build a fire. When he came to the huge rock behind which Palamabron was, he hesitated. He did not want to see what he thought he must when he came around the boulder.

Palamabron had his back to them. He was on his knees before a pile of branches and leaves and was knocking a piece of flint against a rock that was heavy in iron.

Wolff breathed a sigh of relief. The body beside Palamabron was that of a fudger.

Where was Enion?

Wolff came up silently behind Palamabron, his stick raised high. He spoke loudly. "Well, Palamabron?"

The Lord gave a short scream and dived forward over the firepile. He rolled and came up on his feet, facing them. He held a very crude flint knife.

"It's mine," he snarled. "I killed it, and I want it. I have to have it. I'll die if I don't get to eat!"

"So will we all," Wolff said. "Where is your brother?"

Palamabron spit and said, "The beast! He's no brother of mine. How should I know where he is? Why should I care?"

"You went out with him," Wolff said.

"I don't know where he is. We got separated while we were hunting."

"We thought we heard a cry," Vala said.

"It was a fudger, I think," Palamabron said. "Yes, it was. The one I killed a little while ago. I found it sleeping and killed it and it cried out as it died."

"Maybe," Wolff said. He backed away from Palamabron until he was at a safe distance. He continued on up the rivershore. Before he had gone a hundred yards, he saw the hand lying beside a boulder. He went around it and found Enion. The back of his head was crushed in; beside him lay the bloody rock that had killed him.

He returned to Palamabron and Vala. She was still there; the Lord and the fudger were gone.

"Why didn't you stop him?" Wolff said.

She shrugged and smiled. "I'm only a woman. How could I stop him?"

"You could have," he replied. "I think you wanted to enjoy the chase after him. Well, let me tell you, there won't be any. None of us have the strength to waste it climbing around here. And when he eats, he'll have enough strength to outclimb or outrun us."

"Very well," she said. "So what do we do now?"

"Keep on going and hope for the best."

"And starve!" she said. She pointed at the boulder which hid Enion's body. "There's enough food for all of us."

Wolff did not reply for a moment. He had not wanted to think about this, but, since he was faced with it, he would do what had to be done. Vala was right. Without this food, however horrible it was to think about it, they might well die. In a way, Palamabron had done them a favor. He had taken the guilt upon himself of killing for them. They could eat without considering themselves murderers. Not that killing would bother the rest of them. He, however, would have suffered agonies if he had been forced into a position where he had to slay a human being to survive.

As for the actual eating, he was now feeling only a slight repulsion. Hunger had deadened his normal horror against cannibalism.

He returned to wake the others while Vala picked up the rocks dropped by Palamabron. By the time they returned, she had not only started a fire but was intent on the butchering. Wolff held back for a moment. Then, thinking that if he was to share in the food, he should also share in the work, he took Theotormon's knife. The others offered a hand, but he turned them down. It was as if he wanted to punish himself by making himself do most of the grisly work.

When the meal was cooked, half-cooked, rather, he took his share and went around the boulder to eat. He was not sure that he could keep the meat down, and he was sure that if he watched the others eat, he would not be able to keep from vomiting. Somehow, it did not seem so bad if he were alone.

Dawn had found them still cooking. Not until the middle of the morning did they start traveling again. The meat that had not been eaten was wrapped in leaves.

"If Urizen was watching us," Wolff said, "he must really be laughing."

"Let him laugh," Vala said. "My turn will come."

"*Your* turn? You mean, *our* turn."

"You may do what you like. All I'm interested in is what I do."

"Typical of the Lords," said Wolff without elaborating. He watched her for a while after that. She had amazing vitality. Perhaps it was the food that had given her such a swift walk and had filled out her cheeks and arms. He did not think so. Even during the starvation, she had not seemed to suffer as much as the rest or to waste away as swiftly.

If anybody could survive to get at her father's throat, it would be Vala, he thought.

May I not be far behind her, he prayed. *Not so much for vengeance on Urizen, though I want that, as to rescue Chryseis.*

XII

THEY HAD BEEN without food for a day when they emerged from the canyon. Before them, at the foot of a long gentle hill, was a plain that stretched to the horizon. A quarter of a mile away was a small hill, and on this were two giant hexagons.

They stopped to look dully at their goal. Wolff said, "I suggest we take one or the other gate immediately. Perhaps there may be food on the other side."

"If not?" Tharmas said.

"I'd rather die quickly trying to get through Urizen's defenses than starve slowly. Which, at the moment, looks as if it might . . ."

He let his voice trail off, thinking that the Lords felt low enough.

They followed him sluggishly up to the foot of the golden, gem-studded frames. He said to Vala, "Sister, you have the honor of choosing the right or the left entrance for us. Continue. Only be quick about it. I can hear my strength ebbing away."

She picked up a stone, turned her back to the gates, and cast the stone over her head. It sailed through the right gate, almost striking the frame.

"So be it," Wolff said. He looked at them and laughed. "What a crew! Brave Lords! Tramps rather! Sticks, a broken sword, a knife, and muscles shaking with weakness and bellies groaning for meat. Was ever a Lord attacked in his own stronghold by such a contemptible bunch?"

Vala laughed and said, "At least you have some spirit left, Jadawin. That may mean something."

"I hope so," he said, and he ran forward and jumped through the right gate. He came out under a deep-blue sky and onto ground that gave under his feet a little. The topography was flat except for a few steep hills, so rough and dark that they looked more like excrescences than mounds of dirt. He doubted they were dirt, since the surface on which he stood was not earth. It was brownish but smooth and with small holes in it. A foot-high stalk, thin as a pipestem cleaner, grew out of each hole.

Almost like the skin of a giant, he thought.

The only vegetation, if it could be called that, was a number of widely separated trees. These were about forty feet high, were thinly trunked, and had smooth, sharply pointed branches that projected at a forty-five degree angle upwards from the trunk. The branches were darker than the saffron of the main shaft and sparsely covered with blade-like leaves about two feet long.

The other Lords came through the gate a minute later. He turned and said, "I'm glad I didn't find anything I couldn't have handled without your help."

Vala said, "They all were sure that this time the gate would lead into Urizen's stronghold."

"And perhaps I'd trip a few traps before I went down," he said. "And so give the rest of you a chance to live a few minutes longer."

They did not reply. Wolff gazed reproachfully at Luvah, whose cheeks reddened.

Wolff tested the gate. It had either been deactivated or else was unipolar. He saw a long black line that could be the shore of a lake or sea. This world, unlike the one they had just left, gave no indications of the direction they must take. On the side, where he had first stepped, however, he had seen two rough dark hills very close together. These might or not be some sort of sign from Urizen. There was only one way to find out, which Wolff took without hesitation.

He set out on the slightly springy ground, the others trailing. The shadow of a bird passed before them, and they looked up. It was white with red legs, about the size of a bald eagle, and had a monkey face with a curving bird's beak instead of a nose. It swooped so low that Luvah threw his stick at it. The stick passed behind its flaring tail. It squawked indignantly and climbed away swiftly.

Wolff said, "That looks like a nest on that tree. Let's see if it could have eggs."

Luvah ran forward to recover his stick, then stopped. Wolff stared where Luvah was pointing.

The earth was rippling. It rose in inch-high waves and advanced towards the stick. Luvah turned to run, thought better of it, turned again, and ran to pick up the stick. Behind him, the earth swelled, rose up and up, and raced forward, like a surfer's wave.

Wolff yelled. Luvah whirled, saw the danger, and ran away from it. He ran at an angle, towards the end of the wave. Wolff came along behind it, not knowing what he could do to help Luvah but hoping to do something.

Then the wave collapsed. Wolff and Luvah stopped. Abruptly, Wolff felt the earth rising below his feet and saw that another swelling had started some ten feet from Luvah. Both turned and raced away, the earth—or whatever it was—chasing after them.

They made it back to the area around the gate, which had been stable and would continue to be so—they hoped.

They got to the safety zone just in time to escape the sudden sinking of the land behind them. A hole, broad and shallow at first, appeared. Then it narrowed and deepened. The sides closed in on themselves, there was a smacking sound, and the hole reversed its original process. It widened out until all was smooth as before, except that the foot-high, thin growths sprouting from each depression kept on vibrating.

"What in Los' name!" Luvah said over and over. He was pale, and the freckles stood out like a galaxy of fear.

Wolff was a little sick himself. Feeling the earth tremble under him had been like being caught in an earthquake. In fact, that was what he had thought when it first happened.

Somebody yelled behind him. He spun to see Palamabron trying to get back through the gate through which he had just stepped only to go flying vainly through the frame. He must have been following them and waited until he thought they had gone some distance from the gate. Now, he was trapped as much as they.

More so, since Wolff had use for him. Wolff shoved the others away from Palamabron's throat and shouted at them to leave him alone. They drew back while Palamabron shook and his teeth chattered.

"Palamabron," Wolff said, "you have been sentenced to death because you broke truce with us and murdered your brother."

Palamabron, seeing that he was not to be killed out of hand, took courage. Perhaps he thought he had a chance. He cried, "At least I did not eat my own brother! And I had to kill him! He attacked me first!"

"Enion was struck in the back of the head," Wolff said.

"I knocked him down!" Palamabron shouted. "He started to rise when I seized a rock and hit him with it. It was not my fault he had his back turned. Would you ask me to wait until he had turned around?"

"There's no use talking about this," Wolff said. "But you can go free. Your blood will not be on our hands. Only, you can't stay with us. None of us would feel safe to sleep at night or turn our backs on you."

"You are letting me go?" Palamabron said. "Why?"

"Don't waste time talking," Wolff said. "If you don't get out of our sight within ten minutes, I'll let the others at you. You'd better leave. Now!"

"Wait a minute," Palamabron said. "There's something very suspicious about this. No, I won't go."

Wolff gestured at the others. "Go ahead. Kill him."

Palamabron screamed, turned, and ran away as swiftly as he could. He seemed weak, and his legs began to move slowly after the first thirty yards. He looked back several times, then, seeing that they were not coming after him, he quit running.

The earth swelled behind him and built up until it was twice as high as his head. At the moment it gained its peak, Palamabron looked over his shoulder again. He saw the giant wave racing towards him, and he screamed and began to run again. The wave collapsed, the tremors following the collapse upsetting Palamabron and knocking him off his feet. He scrambled up and continued to go on, although he was staggering by now.

A hole opened up ahead of him. He screamed and darted off at right angles to it, seeming to gain new strength from terror. The hole disappeared, but a second gaped ahead of him. Again, he raced away, this time diagonally to the hole.

Another wave began to build up before him. He whirled, slipped, fell hard, rolled over, and stumbled away. Presently, the swelling, which had risen directly between Palamabron and the Lords, grew so high that it walled him off from their sight. After that, the wave froze for a moment, rigid except for a slight trembling. Gradually, it subsided, and the plain was flat again, with the exception of a six-foot long mound.

"Swallowed up," Vala said. She seemed thrilled. Her eyes were wide open, her mouth parted, the lower lip wet. Her tongue flicked out to trace with its tip the oval of both lips.

Wolff said, "Our father has indeed created a monster for us. Perhaps, this entire planet is covered with the skin of . . . of this *Weltthier*."

"What?" said Theotormon. His eyes were still glazed with terror. And though he had been shrinking during the starvation on the last world, he now seemed to have dwindled off fifty pounds in the past two minutes. His skin hung in loops.

"*Weltthier*. World-animal. From German, a Terrestrial language."

A planet covered with skin, he thought. Or maybe it was not so much a skin as a continent-sized amoeba spread out over the globe. The idea made him boggle.

The skin existed; there was no denying that. But how did it keep from starving to death? The millions and millions of tons of protoplasm had to be fed. Certainly, although it ate animals, it could not get nearly enough of these to maintain itself.

Wolff decided to investigate the subject, if he ever got the chance. He was as curious as a monkey or a Siamese cat, always probing, pondering, speculating, and analyzing. He could not rest until he knew the why and how.

He sat down to rest while he considered what to do. The others, Vala excepted, also sat or lay down. She walked from the "safety zone," placing her feet carefully with each step. Watching her, he understood what she was doing. Why had he not thought of that? She was avoiding contact with the plants (hairs?) that grew from the holes (pores?). After traveling on a circle with a radius of about twenty-five yards, she returned to the gate area. Not once had the skin trembled or begun to form threatening shapes.

Wolff stood up and said, "Very good, Vala. You beat me to it. The beast, or whatever it is, detects life by touch through the feelers or hairs. If we navigate as cautiously as ships going through openings in reefs, we can cross over this thing. Only trouble is, how do we get past those?"

He pointed outwards to the horny buttes, the excrescentoid hills. The hairs began to crowd together at their bases, and beyond the buttes they carpeted the ground.

She shrugged and said, "I don't know."

"We'll worry about it when we get to it," he said. He began walking, looking downwards to guide himself among the feelers. The Lords followed him in Indian file, with Vala again being the only exception. She paralleled his course at a distance of five or six yards to his right.

"It's going to be very difficult to hunt animals for food under these conditions," he said. "We'll have to keep one eye on the hairs and one on the animal. A terrible handicap."

"I wouldn't worry," she said. "There may be no animals."

"There is one I'm sure exists," Wolff said. He did not say anything more on the subject although it was evident that Vala was wondering what he meant. He headed towards the "tree" in a branch of which he saw the nest. A circular pile of sticks and leaves, it was lodged at the junction of the trunk and a branch and was about three feet across. The sticks and leaves seemed to be held together with a gluey substance.

He stepped between two feelers, propped his club against the tree, and shinnied up the trunk. Halfway up, he saw the tops of two hexagons on one of the buttes. When he got to the nest, he clung to the trunk with his legs, one arm around the trunk, while with the other hand he poked through leaves on top of the nest. He uncovered two eggs, speckled green and black and about twice the size of turkey eggs. Removing them one by one, he dropped them to Vala.

Immediately thereafter, the mother returned. Larger than a bald eagle, she was white with bluish chevrons, furry, monkey-faced, falcon-beaked, saber-toothed, wolf-eared, bat-winged, archeopteryx-tailed, and vulture-footed.

She shot down on him with wings folded until just before she struck. The wings opened with a whoosh of air, and she screamed like iron being ripped apart. Perhaps the scream was intended to freeze the prey. If so, it failed. Wolff just let loose of the trunk and dropped. Above him came a crash and another scream, this time of frustration and panic, as the beast rammed partly into the nest and partly into the trunk. Evidently, it had expected to have its momentum absorbed by Wolff's body. And it may have underestimated its speed in its fury.

Wolff hit the ground and rolled, knowing that he was disturbing the feelers but unable to prevent it. He came up on his feet, clumps of glued-together sticks and leaves raining around him from the shattered nest. He got to one side just in time to escape being hit by the body of the half-stunned flier. However, the blow would not have been a full one, since the creature had slowed its fall with an instinctive outspreading of wings.

By then, the earth-skin was reacting to the messages transmitted by the feelers. Not only Wolff had contacted them. The other Lords had scattered when Wolff fell, and they had brushed against hairs all around the tree.

"Back to the tree," Wolff yelled at them. Vala had anticipated his advice; she was already halfway up the trunk. He began shinnying after Vala, only to feel talons sharp and hot as glowing-white hooks fasten into his back. The flying beast had recovered and was at him again. Once more, he let loose and fell backward. He kicked his feet against the trunk and shoved out to throw himself into a horizontal attitude. And so he came down hard but with the beast below him.

Two breaths whooshed out, his and that of the beast crushed beneath him. Less hurt, Wolff rolled off, stood up, and kicked the thing in the ribs. Its mouth gaped beneath the brownish beak, its two saber teeth covered with saliva and blood. Wolff kicked again and turned back to the tree. He was bowled over by two Lords frantic to get to the safety of the tree. Tharmas stepped on his head and used it as a springboard to leap for the trunk. Rintrah pulled him down, shoved him away, and started to climb. Staggering back from the push, Tharmas fell over Wolff, who was just getting to his hands and knees.

From her perch near the top of the tree, Vala was laughing hysterically. She laughed and pounded her thigh and then, suddenly, shrieked. Her hold lost, she fell hard, broke off a branch, turned over, and came down on her shoulder. She lay stunned at the base of the tree.

Theotormon was perhaps the most terrified. Still huge despite the many pounds of fat that had thawed off him, and handicapped by having flippers, he had a hard time scaling the tree. He kept slipping back down, the while he could not refrain from looking over his shoulder and gibbering.

Wolff managed to get to his feet. Around him, around the tree, rather, the skin was going mad. It rose in great waves that chased after Luvah and

Ariston. These two were going around in circles with great speed, their fright giving their weary and hungry bodies fresh strength. Behind them, the earth-flesh rose up, moved swiftly after them, then began to curl over. Other waves appeared ahead of them, and pits yawned beneath their feet.

Suddenly, Luvah and Ariston passed each other, and the various moving tumors and depressions hot on their heels collided. Wolff was confused by the chaos of tossing, bumping, smacking, gulping shapes of protoplasm. More than anything, the scene resembled a collection of maelstroms.

Before the skin could get its signals straight and reorganize, it had lost Ariston and Luvah. They gained the trunk of the tree, but they impeded each other's ascent. While they were clawing at each other, Wolff picked up the body of the flier and hurled it from him as far as he could. It landed on an advancing swell, which stopped the moment it detected the carcass. A depression appeared around and beneath the body. Slowly, it sank until it was below the surface. Then the lips of the hole closed over it, and there was only a mound and a seam to show what was beneath.

The flier had been a sacrifice, since Wolff had wanted to keep the body for food. The area around the tree smoothed out, made a few ripples, and became as inert as if it were truly made of earth. Wolff went around the tree to examine Vala. She was sitting up, breathing hard, her face twisted with pain. Since the skin was springy, the impact had not been as hard as if it had occurred on hard dirt. She was bruised on her shoulder and the side of her face, and for a while she could not move her arm.

Her worst injury seemed to be to her dignity. She cursed them for a pack of cowardly fools and males fit only to be slaves—if that. The Lords were abashed by her insults or sullen. They felt that she was right; they were ashamed. But they were certainly not going to admit the truth.

Wolff began to think the whole affair had been funny. He started laughing, then straightened up with a groan. He had forgotten the gashes inflicted by the flier's talons. Luvah looked at his back and clucked. The blood was still oozing out, although he expected that it would soon stop flowing. He certainly hoped that Wolff would not become infected, since there was no medicine to be had.

"You're very cheerful," Wolff growled. He looked around for the eggs. One was smashed and spread over the base of the tree. The other was nowhere in sight and presumably had been swallowed by the skin.

"Oh, Los!" moaned Ariston. "What do we do now? We're about to die of hunger; we're lost; we can't leave this tree without being swallowed alive by that monster. Our father has killed us, and we have not even gotten close to his stronghold."

"You Lords and Makers of Universes are pitiful creatures indeed when stripped of your fortress walls and your weapons," Wolff said. "I'll tell you another old Earth proverb. There's more than one way to skin a cat."

"What cat? Where?" Theotormon said. "I could eat a dozen cats right now."

Wolff rolled his eyes upwards but did not answer. He told the others either to get on the other side of the tree or go up it. Then he took Theotormon's knife and went out a few feet from the tree. Squatting, he jammed the knife with all his strength into the skin. If it was flexible enough to shape itself into rough pseudopods or holes, it had to be vulnerable.

He snatched the knife out of the wound and rose and retreated a few steps. The skin shrank away, became a hole, then a cone formed around the wound, and the cone thrust up, like a crater slowly building itself. Wolff stood patiently. Soon the crater flattened out, and the wound was revealed. Instead of the blood he had been half-expecting, a thin pale liquid oozed out.

He approached the wound, taking care to avoid the hairs near it. Quickly he slashed at the skin again, dug out a quivering mass of flesh, and ran back to the tree. There was a storm of protoplasmic shapes once more: waves, craters, ridges, and brief swirlings in which the flesh formed corkscrew pillars. Then it subsided.

Wolff said, "The skin immediately around the tree seems to be tougher and less flexible than that further away. I think we're safe as long as we stand on it, although the skin might be capable of a . . . a tidal wave that could sweep us off. Anyway, we can eat."

The other Lords took turns cutting out chunks. The raw flesh was tough, slimy with ichor, and ill-smelling, but it could be chewed and swallowed. With something in their bellies, they felt stronger and more optimistic. Some lay down to sleep; Wolff walked to the shore. Vala and Theotormon followed him, and Luvah, seeing them, decided to go along. The land area ended abruptly with no beach for transition. Along the edge there were so few feelers they could relax a little. Wolff stood on the very edge and looked into the water. Despite the fact that there was no sun to cast its beams, the clear water allowed him to see quite deep into it.

There were many fish of various sizes, shapes, and colors swimming close to shore. Even as he watched, he saw a long slender pale tentacle shoot out from under the edge and seize a large fish. The fish struggled but was drawn quickly back under the edge. Wolff got down on all fours and leaned out over the edge to see what kind of creature it was that had caught the prey. The rim on which he stood extended out quite far. In fact, he could not see the base of the land. Instead, he saw a mass of writhing tentacles, many of which gripped fish. And farther back were tentacles that hung deep into the abyss. Presently, one coiled upon itself and brought up a gigantic fish from the deeps.

He withdrew his head hastily, since one of the nearby tentacles was snaking out and up in his general direction. He said, "I wondered how such a monster could get enough to eat. It must feed mainly on the sea life. And I'll bet that this animal on which we stand is a vast floater. Like the islands of the waterworld, this thing is free, unattached to any base."

"That's nice to know," Luvah said. "But how does that help us?"

"We need more to eat," Wolff replied. "Theotormon, you're the swimmer among us. Would you jump in and swim around a bit? Stay close to shore and be ready to shoot back in. Come out fast, like a seal."

Theotormon said, "Why should I? You saw how those tentacles grabbed those fish."

"I think they're grabbing blindly. Maybe they can detect vibrations in the water, I don't know. But you're fast enough to evade them. And the tentacles immediately under this edge are small."

Theotormon shook his head. "No, I won't risk my life for you."

"You'll starve if you don't," Wolff said. "We can't keep on cutting out chunks of skin. It gets too violent."

He pointed at a fish that was just skimming by below the surface. It was fat and sluggish with a head shaped like a sphinx. ''Wouldn't you like to sink your teeth in that?''

Theotormon drooled, and his belly thundered, but he would not go after it.

''Give me your knife, then,'' Wolff said. He removed the weapon from its scabbard before Theotormon, standing on one leg, could lift the other to clutch the hilt with his toes. He turned and ran and dived out as far as he could. The fish wheeled away from him and scooted away. It was slow but not so slow that he could catch it. Nor had he thought he could. He was interested in finding out if a tentacle, feeling the vibrations of the splash and his strokes, would come probing for him.

One did. It undulated down from the fleshy base to which it was attached and then out towards him. He swam back towards the shore, dipping his head below the water to watch it. When he saw it suddenly gain speed as it neared him, he reached out one hand and grabbed its tip. Until then, he had not been certain that the tentacle was not poisonous, like a jellyfish's. However, the fish that had been seized had fought vigorously with no indication of being envenomed.

The tentacle doubled up on itself, looped, and went around him. He released the tip, turned, and grabbed the tentacle about twelve inches back from its tip. He began to saw at the skin with the knife, which went through fairly easy. The tentacle abandoned its efforts to wrap itself around him and began to pull back. He kept hold with one hand and continued to cut. The water became darker as he was carried back under the edge. Then, the knife was through, and he was swimming back up with the severed part in his teeth.

He heaved the tentacle up on shore and was beginning to pull himself out when he felt something enfold his right foot. He looked down at a mouth on the end of another tentacle. The mouth was toothless but strong enough to keep its grip on his foot. He clung with his arms on the edge and gasped, "Help me!"

Theotormon took a few steps towards him on his rubbery legs and then halted. Vala looked down at the thing and smiled. Luvah snatched the broken sword from her scabbard and went into the water. At that, Vala laughed, and she followed Luvah in. She came back up, took Wolff's dagger, and dived back down. She and Luvah went to work on the tentacle a few feet from the mouth. The shaft parted; Wolff pulled himself on out with the amputated mouth-part still ensocked on his foot.

The two pieces of flesh could be eaten only after being pounded against the treetrunk to tenderize them. Even then, eating them was almost like chewing on rubber. But it was more food in the stomach.

Afterwards, they advanced gingerly over the plain. At the point by the first butte, where the hairs began to cluster thickly, they halted. Now they could see their goal. A half-mile away, on top of a tall butte, was the pair of golden hexagons.

Wolff had picked up the branch that Vala's fall had broken off. He threw this hard as he could and watched it come down in the hairs. The whole area reacted at once and far more violently than the less haired area. The skin stormed.

"Oh, Los!" Ariston said. "We're done for! We could never get across that." He shook his fist at the sky and shouted, "You, our father! I hate you! I loathe you, and abominate the day that you jetted me from your foul loins! You may think you have us where you want us! But, by Los and crooked Enitharmon, I swear that we'll get to you yet!"

"That's the spirit," Wolff said. "For a moment, I thought you were going to whine like a sick dog. Tell the old bastard off! He can probably hear you."

Ariston, breathing hard, fists still clenched, said, "Brave enough talk. But I still would like to know what to do."

Wolff said to the others, "Any ideas?"

They shook their heads. He said, "Where is all the diabolical cleverness and weasel agility of mind that the children of Urizen are supposed to have? I've heard tales of each one of you, of how you have assailed the stronghold of many a Lord and by your wits and powers have taken his universe from him. What is the matter now?"

Vala said, "They were brave enough and clever enough when they had their weapons. But I think they're still recovering from the shock of being taken so easily by our father. And of being deprived of their devices. Without those, they lose that which made them Lords. Now, they're only men, and pretty sorry men at that."

"We're so tired," Rintrah said. "My muscles ache and burn. They sag as if I were on a heavy planet."

"Muscles!" Wolff said. "Muscles!"

He led them back to the tree. Despite the flame in his back every time he pulled on a branch—agony from the talon-wounds—he worked with a will. The other Lords helped him, and each soon had a bundle of branches in his arms. They returned to the rim of the overgrown area and here began to cast the sticks as far out into the feelers as they could. They did not do it all at once but spaced their throws. The skin reared up like a sea in a hurricane. Waves, craters, wavelets coursed back and forth.

But as the skin continued to be activated, its ragings became less. Near the end of the supply of branches, it began to react feebly. The last stick got no more than a shallow hole and a weak and quickly subsiding wave.

Wolff said, "It's tired now. Its rate of recovery may be very swift, however. So I suggest we get going now."

He led the way, walking swiftly. The skin quivered and humped up in response to the warnings from the feelers and broad three-or-four-inch deep holes appeared. Wolff skirted them, then decided he should trot. He did not stop until he had reached the foot of the butte. This, like the first they had passed, seemed to be an excrescence, a huge wart on the skin. Though its sides rose perpendicularly, it was wrinkled enough to give hand and footholds. The ascent was not easy but was not impossible. They all got to the top without mishap.

Wolff said, "Yours is the honor again, Vala. Which gate?"

Ariston said, "She hasn't done very well so far. Why let her pick it?"

Vala turned on him like a tigress. "Brother, if you think you can do any better, you choose! But you should show your confidence in yourself by being the first to go through the gate!"

Ariston stepped back and said, "Very well. No use breaking with the custom."

Vala said, "So it's a custom now! Well, I choose the left one."

Wolff did not hesitate. Although he felt that this time he might find himself, weak and weaponless, in Urizen's fortress, he stepped through.

For a moment, he could not understand where he was or what was happening, he was so dizzy and the objects that hurtled above him were so strange.

XIII

HE WAS ON a huge gray metallic cylinder that was rotating swiftly. Above him, on both sides, and also coming into view as the cylinder whirled, were other gray cylinders. The sky behind them was a pale pink.

Between each of the cylinders were three glowing beams of mauve light. These began about ten feet from the ends of the cylinders and from the middle. Every now and then, colored lights burst along the lengths of the beams and ran up and down them. Red, orange, black, white, purple, they burst like Very lights and then bobbed along the beams as if jerked along by an invisible cord. When they came to a point about twelve feet from the cylinders, they flared brightly and quickly died out.

Wolff closed his eyes to fight off the dizziness and the sickness. When he opened them again, he saw that the others had come through the gates. Ariston and Tharmas fell to the surface and clung as tightly as they could. Theotormon sat down as if he feared the spinning would send him scooting across the metal or perhaps might hurl him out into the space between the cylinders. Only Vala seemed not to be affected. She was smiling, although it could have been a mere show of courage.

If so, she was to be admired for achieving even this.

Wolff studied the environment as best he could. The cylinders were all about the size of skyscrapers.

Wolff did not understand why they were not all spun off immediately by centrifugal force. Surely, these bodies could not have much gravity.

Yet, they did.

Perhaps—no perhaps—Urizen had set up a balance of forces which enabled objects with such strong gravities to keep from falling on each other. Perhaps the colored lights that ran along the beams were manifestations of the continual rebalancing of whatever statics and dynamics were being used to maintain the small but Earth-heavy bodies.

Wolff did not know anything except that the science that the Lords had inherited was far beyond that which Terrestrials knew.

There must be thousands, perhaps hundreds of thousands, of these cylinders. They were about a mile apart from each other, spinning on their own axes and also shifting slowly about each other in an intricate dance.

From a distance, Wolff thought, the separate bodies would look like one solid bulk. This must be one of the planets he had observed from the water-world.

There was one advantage to their predicament. On a world as tiny as this one, they would not have to go far to find the next set of gates. But it did not seem likely that Urizen would make things so easy for them.

Wolff stepped back to the gate and tried to reenter it. As he had expected, it only permitted him to step through the frame and back onto the cylinder. He turned and tested its other side, only to find that equally unfruitful. Then he set out to look for the gates by walking around the circumference. And when he had gotten less than halfway around, he saw the two hexagons.

These were at one end and hung a few inches above the surface, the pale sky gleaming pinkly between the lower frame and the cylinder surface. With the others, he set out to walk towards it. He kept his eyes on the gates and tried not to see the whirling shifting objects around him.

Wolff was in the lead and so was the first to notice the unexpected behavior of the twin hexagons. As he came within fifty feet of them, they began to move away. He increased his pace; the gates did not maintain quite the same distance. When he broke into a run, they went more swiftly but still he gained a little. He stopped; the gates stopped. He made a dash at them, only to see them start off just as quickly. As he stepped up his speed, he gained on them.

The other Lords were behind him. Their feet slapped on the metallic surface, and their gaspings whistled through the atmosphere. Wolff stopped again. The gates halted. The other Lords, except Vala, gathered around him and babbled.

"Los! First he starves us to death . . . then runs us to death."

Wolff waited until he had recovered his breath, then said, "I think they can be caught. They began to slow down in their speed as I went faster. It's a proportional decrease. But I don't think I can go quickly enough and long enough to catch them. Who's the fastest here?"

Luvah said, "I could always beat the rest of you in a foot race. But now I am so tired and weak . . ."

"Try," Wolff said.

Luvah grinned uncertainly at him and inched towards the gates. Hovering, they moved away. He broke into a dash and presently was gone around the curve of the cylinder out of their sight. Wolff turned and ran in the opposite direction. After him came Vala. The dizzyingly close horizon jumped at him; he sped on and then he saw Luvah and the gates. Luvah was now within ten feet of them, but he was slowing down. And as his legs refused to move as he wished and his breath burned out of his lungs, the gates drew away.

Wolff came up behind the gates. When he was as close to them as Luvah, the gates slipped sideways, like

wet soap between two hands. Vala came in at an angle
towards them, but they veered off. The panting Lords
stopped, forming three corners of a square with the gates
at the remaining corner.

"Where are the others?" Wolff said.

Luvah jerked a thumb. Wolff looked around to see
them straggling around the curve of this minute world.
He called to them, his voice sounding eerie in the
strangely propertied atmosphere. Luvah started to go
forward but stopped at Wolff's order.

Ariston, Tharmas, Rintrah, and Theotormon spread
out. Under Wolff's directions, they formed a pentagon
with the gates at the ends of two legs of the figure. Then
all began to close in on their quarry. They kept the same
distance between them and advanced at the same pace.
The gates oscillated back and forth but made no break.

With two minutes of slow and patient closing in, the
Lords were able to seize half of the frames. This time,
Wolff did not bother to ask Vala which exit they should
take. He went through the left.

The others came through on his heels and their look of
dismay reflected his. They were on another cylinder,
and down at the end was another pair of hexagons.

Again, they went through the tiring chase and the
boxing in. Again, they stepped through a frame, the one
to the right this time. Again, they were on another
cylinder.

This occurred five times. The Lords looked at each
other with fatigue-reddened and exhaustion-circled
eyes. Their legs trembled, and their chests ached. They
were covered with sweat and were as dry within as a
Saharan wind. They could hardly keep their grips on the
hexagons.

"We can't go on much longer," Rintrah said.

"Don't be so obvious," Vala said. "Try to say something original once in a while."

"Very well. I'm thirsty enough to drink your blood.

And I may if I don't get a drink of water soon.''

Vala laughed. ''If you come close enough, I'll broach you with this sword. Your blood may be thin and ill-smelling, but at least it should be wet enough.''

Wolff said, ''Somehow, we always seem to take the gate that leads us everywhere but to Urizen. Perhaps we should split up this time. At least some might get to our father.''

The others argued about this, Vala and Luvah only abstaining. Finally, Wolff said, ''I'm going through one gate with Vala and Luvah. The rest of you will go through the other. That's that.''

''Why Vala and Luvah?'' Theotormon said. He was squinting suspiciously, and his voice had a faint whine. ''Why them? Do you three know something we don't? Are you planning on deserting us?''

''I'm taking Luvah because he's the only one I can trust—I think,'' Wolff said. ''And Vala is, as she's pointed out more than enough times, the best man among you.''

He left them squabbling and, with his sister and Luvah, went through the left gate. A few minutes later, the others came through. They looked bewildered on seeing Wolff, Luvah, and Vala.

''But we went through the right-hand gate,'' Rintrah said.

Vala laughed and said, ''Our father has played us another grim jest. Both gates of a pair lead to the same cylinder. I suspect that they all will.''

''He's not playing fair!'' Ariston said. At this, Wolff and Luvah laughed, and presently the others, Ariston excepted, had joined him in his mirth.

When the howling—which had a note of despair in it—had died, Wolff said, ''I may be wrong. But I think that every one of these thousands of cylinders in this— this *birling* world—has a set of gates. And if we continue the same behavior, we'll go through every one of them.

Only we'll die before we get a fraction of the way. We must think of something new.''

There was a silence. They sat or lay on the hard gray shiny metal while they whirled around, the cylinders above them rotated about each other in a soundless and intricate saraband, and the twin hexagons at the end hovered and seemed to mock.

Finally, Vala said, ''I do not think that we have been left without a way out. It would not be like our father to stop the game while we still have an atom of breath and of fight in us. He would want to drag out the agony until we broke. And I'm sure that he plans on allowing us eventually to find the gate that will conduct us into his stronghold. He must be planning some choice receptions for us, and he would be disappointed if he could not use them.

''So, I think that we have not been using our wits. Obviously, these gates lead only to other sets on other cylinders. That is, they do if we go through the regular way, through the side which is set with jewels. But what if the gates are bipolar? What if the other side would take us where we want to go?''

Wolff said, ''I tested the other side when we first came through.''

''Yes, you tested the initial gate. But have you tested any of the double gates?''

Wolff shook his head and said, ''Exhaustion and thirst are robbing me of my wits. I should have thought of that. After all, it's the only thing left to try.''

''Then let's up and at them,'' Vala said. ''Summon your strength; this may be our exit from this cursed birling world.''

Once more, they corraled the twin hexagons and seized them. Vala was the first to go through the side opposite the gem-set side. She disappeared, and Wolff followed her. On coming through and seeing another cylinder, he felt his spirits dissipate like wine in a vacuum Then he saw the gate at the end and knew that they had taken the correct route.

There was only one golden hexagon. It, too, hovered a few inches above the surface. But it spun on its axis, around and around, completing a cycle every second and a half.

The others came through and cursed when they realized that they were still on a birling. But when they saw the single rotating gate, some brightened up; others sagged at the thought of facing a new peril.

"Why does it whirl?" Ariston said weakly.

"I really can't say, brother," Vala said. "But, knowing Father, I would suspect that the gate has only one safe side. That is, if we choose the right side, we'll go through unharmed. But if we take the wrong side . . . You'll observe that neither side has jewels; both are bare. So there's no way of distinguishing one side from another."

"I am so weary I do not care," Ariston said. "I would welcome death. To sleep forever, free of this agony of body and mind, that is all I desire."

"If you really feel that way," Vala said, "then you should be the first to test the gate."

Wolff said nothing, but the others added their voices to Vala's urgings. Ariston did not seem so eager to die now; he objected, saying that he was not fool enough to sacrifice himself for them.

"You are not only a weakling but a coward, brother," Vala said. "Very well, I will be the first."

Stung, Ariston started towards the spinning hexagon but stopped when a few feet from it. He stared at it and continued to stand motionless while Vala jeered him. She shoved him to one side so hard he staggered and fell on the gray surface. Then she crouched before the golden cycler and studied it intently for several minutes. Suddenly, she launched herself forward and went through the opening headfirst. The gate whirled on around.

Ariston arose without looking at the others or replying to their taunts. He walked up to the gate, bent his knees, and dived through.

And he came out on the other side and fell on the gray surface.

Wolff, the first to him, turned him over.

Ariston's mouth hung open; his eyes were glazing; his skin was turning gray.

Wolff stood up and said, "He went through the wrong side. Now we know what kind of gate this is."

"That bitch Vala has all the luck!" Tharmas said. "Did you notice which side she went through?"

Wolff shook his head. He studied the frame in the pink dusk. There were no markings of any kind on either side to distinguish one from the other. He spoke to Luvah, and they picked up Ariston's body by the feet and shoulders. They swung it back and forth until, at Wolff's shout, they released the corpse at the height of its forward swing. It shot through the frame and came out on the other side and fell on the surface.

Wolff and Luvah went to the other side and once more swung his body and then cast it through the frame. This time it did not reappear. Wolff said to Rintrah, "Are you counting?"

Rintrah nodded his head. Wolff said, "Lift your finger, and when the right side comes around, point it. Do it swiftly!"

Rintrah waited until two more turns had been made, then stabbed his finger. Wolff hurled himself through the frame, hoping that Rintrah had not made a mistake. He landed on Ariston's body. There was the sound of sea and a red sky above. Vala was standing nearby and laughing softly as if she were actually enjoying their father's joke.

They were back on an island of the waterworld.

XIV

THE OTHER Lords came through the gate one by one, Rintrah last. They did not look downcast as might have been expected. At least, they were on familiar grounds, almost home, one might say. And, as Theotormon did say, they could eat all they wanted.

The gate through which they had entered was the right one of an enormous pair. Both stood on a low hill. The immediate terrain looked familiar. After the Lords had gone to the shore to quench their thirst, they cooked and ate the fish that Theotormon caught. They set up a guard-rotation system and slept. The next day, they explored.

There was no doubt that they were back on the great island the natives called the "Mother of Islands."

"Those gates are the same ones that started us off on the not-so-merry-go-round," Wolff said. "We went through the right-hand one. So, the left one may lead to Urizen's world."

Tharmas said, "Perhaps . . . well, this is not the most desirable of worlds. But it is better to enjoy life here than to die or live in pain in one of Urizen's cells. Why not forget that gate? There is food and water here and native women. Let Urizen sit in his seat of power forever and rot waiting for us to come to him."

"You forget that, without your drugs, you will get old and will die," Wolff said. "Do you want that? Moreover, there is no guarantee that Urizen will not come to us if we don't go to him. No, you may sit here in a lotus-eater's dream if you want, but I intend to keep fighting."

"You see, Tharmas," Vala said, smiling crookedly. "Jadawin has stronger reasons than we do. His woman—who is not a Lord, by the way, but an inferior breed from Earth—is a prisoner of Urizen's. He cannot rest while he knows she is in our father's hands.''

''It's up to you to do what you want,'' Wolff said. ''But I am my own master.''

He studied the red heavens, the two huge-seeming planets that were in sight at this time, and a tiny streak that could have been a black comet. He said, ''Why go through the front door, where Urizen expects us? Why not sneak through the back door? Or, a better metaphor, through a window?''

In answer to their questions, he explained the idea that had come to him when he looked at the other planets and the comet. They replied that he was crazy. His concepts were too fantastic.

''Why not?'' he said. ''As I've said, everything we need can be gotten, even if we have to go through the gates again. And Appirmatzum is only twenty-five thousand miles away. Why can't we get there with the ship I proposed?''

''A balloon spacecraft?'' Rintrah said. ''Jadawin, your life on Earth has addled your wits!''

''I need the help of every one of you,'' Wolff said. ''It's an undertaking of large magnitude and complexity. It'll take tremendous labors and a long time. But it can be done.''

Vala said, ''Even if it can be accomplished, what's to prevent our father from detecting our craft as it comes through the space between this world and his?''

''We'll have to take the chance that he's not set up detectors for spacecraft. Why should he? The only entrance to this universe is through the gate that he made himself.''

''But what if one of us is a traitor?'' she said. ''Have you thought that one of us may be in Urizen's service and so spying for him?''

"Of course I've considered that. So has every one else. However, I can't see a traitor putting himself through the extreme dangers that we just went through."

"And how do we know that Urizen is not seeing and hearing everything right now?" Theotormon said.

"We don't. That's another chance we'll have to take."

"It's better than doing nothing," Vala said.

There was much argument after that with all the Lords finally agreeing to help him in his plan. Even the objectors knew that if Wolff succeeded, those who refused to aid him would be marooned on this island. The thought that their brothers might be true Lords again while the objectors would be no better than the natives was too much for them.

The first thing Wolff did was to find out the temper of the neighboring natives. To his surprise, he found that they were not hostile. They had seen the Lords disappear into the gate and then come out again. Only the gods or demigods could do this; therefore, the Lords must be special—and dangerous—creatures. The natives were more than happy to cooperate with Wolff. Their religion, a debased form of the Lords' original religion, determined this decision. They believed in Los as the good God and in Urizen as the evil one, their version of Satan. Their prophets and medicine men maintained that some day the evil one, Urizen, would be overthrown. When that happened, they would all go to Alulos, their heaven.

Wolff did not try to set them straight on the facts. Let them believe what they wished as long as they helped him. He set everybody to work on the things that could be done immediately and with materials available on this world. Then, he went through the gate that led to the other planets. Luvah went with him. Both were buoyed up by gas-bladders strapped to their backs and armed with short spears and bows and arrows. Through gate after gate they traveled, searching for the things that Wolff needed. They knew what to expect and what dangers to avoid. Even so, the adventures they met on this trip and the many trips thereafter were enough to have filled several books. But there were no more casualties.

Later, Vala and Rintrah accompanied Wolff and Luvah. They brought back chunks of the vitreous stuff from the world of the skating and suction-pad animals. From the Welt thier, they brought back piles of bird-droppings. These, added to the store of their own and the natives' excrement, were to provide the sodium nitrate crystals in Wolff's plan.

The mercury was gotten from the natives, who had large supplies picked up from the island after the showers that came with the black comets. The mercury droplets were religious objects and were given to Wolff only after he argued that they were to be used against Urizen. He discovered that one of the plants on the island was a source of wood alcohol. Other plants could be burned to give the charcoal he needed. And the planet of the tempusfudgers furnished sulphur.

Wolff had to have a platinum catalyst in the making of nitric acid. While on the cylinders of the birling world, he had thought that the cylinders might be composed of platinum or of a platinum alloy. This metal had a melting point of 1773.5 Centigrade and was resistant to cutting. Wolff had no means to melt it in the birling world or any tools sharp enough to cut out chunks from a cylinder. Luvah pointed this out, to which Wolff replied that they would use Urizen's own devices for the job.

He took all the Lords with him, even though

Theotormon and Tharmas strongly objected. They cornered the mobile twin gates and then pulled them to the edge of the cylinder. Here Theotormon found out why it was necessary for him to make the trip. His weight was needed to force the gates halfway down over the arc of the edge of the cylinder. The forces that kept the gates upright were strong but could not resist the combined weight and muscles of the Lords.

A portion of the arc went through one of the gates. Had the gate been held motionless, the piece of the cylinder would merely have projected through its matching gate on another cylinder. But when the gate was pulled sidewise along the edge, something had to give. The gate acted like a shears and cut off the part which went through the frame.

After setting the gate upright, the Lords went through it to the next cylinder, where they found a chunk of the platinum. And they used the next gate to cut the chunk into smaller pieces.

On the cylinder of the whirling death-gate, Wolff tested it with several stones. As soon as a stone disappeared, he marked the safe side with a dab of yellow paint brought from the waterworld. Thereafter, they had no trouble distinguishing the death-side from the safe side.

Wolff had the gates that could be moved in the various worlds transported to a more advantageous location.

The island on the waterworld became one vast forge of smoke and stink. The Lords and the natives complained mightily. Wolff listened, scoffed, laughed, or threatened, as the occasion demanded. He drove them on. Three hundred and sixty dark moons passed. The work was slow, disappointing many times, and often dangerous. Wolff and Luvah kept on making trips through the gates, bringing back from the still perilous circuit the materials they needed.

By this time the balloon spacecraft was half-built. When finished, it would ascend with the Lords until it rose above the atmosphere. Here the pseudogravity field weakened rapidly—if Theotormon was to be believed—and the craft would use the drag of the dark moon to pick up more speed. Then blackpowder rockets would give it more velocity. And steering would be done through small explosions of power or through release of gas-jets from bladders.

The gondola would be airtight. Wolff had not yet worked out the problem of air-renewal and circulation or the other problems brought on by nongravity. Actually, they should have a certain amount of gravity. They would not be getting into space as a rocket does, which attains escape velocity. Levitated by the expanding gas in the lift-bladders, they would rise until the atmosphere gave out. One past the atmosphere, the craft would lose its buoyancy, and would have to depend upon the pull of the moon and the weak reaction of wooden-cased rockets to give them thrust enough to escape the waterworld's grip.

Moreover, if they did pull lose from the waterworld, they would be in danger of being seized by the field of the moon.

"There's no way of determining the proper escape path and necessary vectors by mathematics," Wolff said to Luvah. "We'll just have to play it by ear."

"Let's hope we're not tone-deaf," Luvah said. "Do you think we really have a chance?"

"With what I have in mind, I think there is," Wolff replied. "Just now, today, I want to think of other things. There are the spacesuits to work on for instance. We'll have to wear them while in the gondola, since we can't rely on the gondola being too airtight."

The fulminate of mercury for the explosive caps was made. This was a dark-brown powder formed by reaction of mercury, alcohol, and concentrated nitric acid.

The nitric acid, which oxidized sulfur to sulfuric acid, was obtained through a series of steps. The sodium nitrate, gotten by crystallization from the bird droppings and human excrement, was heated with sulfuric acid. (The sulfuric acid was derived by burning sulfur with saltpeter, that is, potassium or sodium nitrate.)

Free nitrogen of the air was "fixed" by combining it with hydrogen (from the gas bladders) to form ammonia. The ammonia was mixed with oxygen (from an oxygen-producing bladder) at the correct temperature. The mixture was passed over a fine wire gauge made from smooth compact platinum to catalyze for catalysis.

The resulting nitrogen oxides were absorbed in water; the dilute acid was gotten by concentration through distillation.

The materials for the furnaces and containers and pipes were furnished by the vitreous stuff from the planet of skaters.

Black gunpowder was made from charcoal, sulfur, and the saltpeter.

Wolff also succeeded in making ammonium nitrate, a blasting power of considerable power.

One day Vala said, "Don't you think that you're making far too many explosives? We can't take more than a fraction on the ship. Otherwise, the ship'll never get off the ground."

"That's true," he replied. "Maybe you were also wondering why I've stocked the explosives at widely separated locations. That's because gunpowder is unstable. If one pile goes up, the others won't be affected."

Some of the Lords paled. Rintrah said. "You mean the explosives we'll be taking on the ship could go off at any time?"

"Yes. That's one more chance we'll be taking. None of this is easy or safe, you know. But I'd like to add a possibly cheering note. It is ironic and laughable, if we succeed, that Urizen himself has supplied the materials for his own undoing. He has furnished us with the basic weapons which might overthrow his supertechnology."

"If we live, we'll laugh," Rintrah said. "I think, however, that Urizen will be the laugher."

"Old Earth proverb: We'll at least give him a run for his money. Another proverb: He who laughs last laughs best."

That night Wolff went to Luvah's hut. Luvah woke up swiftly on feeling Wolff's hand on his shoulder. He started to draw the knife made of flint from the tempusfudger planet. Wolff said, "I'm here to talk, not kill. Luvah, you are the only one I can trust to help me. And I need help."

"I am honored, brother. You are by far the best man among us. And I know that you are not about to propose treachery."

"Part of what I plan may seem at first to be treachery. But it is necessary. Listen carefully, young brother."

Within the hour, they left the hut. Carrying digging and hacking tools, they went to the hill on which stood the twin gates. Here they were met by twenty natives, all of whom Wolff was sure he could trust. They began cutting and digging through the tangle of decayed vegetation and bladder roots that formed the island. All worked swiftly and hard, so that by the time the moon had passed and taken night with it, they had completed a trench around the hill. They kept on working until there was only a few inches of roots to go before coming to the water level. Then the natives placed ammonium nitrate and fulminate caps in the trench. When this was done, they threw in the chopped up roots and dirt and made an attempt to cover the signs of excavation.

"Anybody can see at a glance that digging has been done here," Wolff said. "I'm banking on nobody coming here, however. I told all of you that today would be a rest day so that you wouldn't rise until late."

He looked at the gates. "Now you and I must travel the circuit again. And we must do it swiftly."

When they came to the planet of the tempus-fudgers, Wolff gave Luvah one of his blowguns. This was made of the hollow bamboo-like plants that grew on the mother-island. The natives used them to shoot darts tipped with a stupefacient made from a certain species of fish. They hunted the birds and the rats on the island with these.

Wolff and Luvah went into a canyon and there knocked out five of the fudgers. Wolff searched until he found the entrance to a burrow in which chronowolves lived. He placed the end of the blowgun inside the burrow and expelled the dart. After waiting a minute, he reached in and dragged out a sleeping wolf.

The animals, still unconscious, were cast into the gate that would open into Urizen's world. Or it should lead there. It was possible that both gates merely led to the next secondary planet, as the gates on the birling world had.

"I hope the little animals will trigger off Urizen's alarms," Wolff said. "The alarms will keep him busy for a while. There's also the possibility that the fudgers' and wolf's time-leaping and duplicating abilities will enable them to survive for a while. They may even multiply and spread through the palace and set off any number of traps and alarms. Urizen won't know what the hell's going on. And he'll be diverted from the gate through which he expected us to come."

"You don't know that," Luvah said. "Both these gates here, and both those on the waterworld, may just lead to another secondary."

"Nothing's certain in any of the multitudinous universes," Wolff said. "And even for the immortal Lords, Death waits around every corner. So let's go around the corner."

They passed through the gate into the Weltthier. There was no sign of the chronobeasts. Wolff took heart at this, thinking that the chances were very good that the animals had gone into Urizen's stronghold.

Back upon the waterworld, Luvah went off to accomplish his mission. Wolff watched him go. Perhaps he had been wrong in suspecting Vala of alliance with her father. But she had been too lucky in getting to a safe place whenever danger threatened. She had acted too quickly. Moreover, when they were in the river of the icerock planet, she had been too buoyant and just a little too assured. He suspected that the girdle around her waist contained devices to enable her to float. And there was the choosing of the gates by her. Every time, these had led to a secondary. They should have gone through one of Urizen's gates at least once. She had been too self-assured, even for her. It was as if she were playing a game.

Although she hated her father, she could have joined him to bring her brothers and cousins to death. She hated them as much as she hated her father. She could have transceivers implanted in her body. Thus, Urizen would be able to hear, and probably to see, all that she did. She would enjoy the game as a participant, perversely enjoy it even more if she were in some danger herself.

Urizen could take pleasure in the deadly games as if he were watching a TV set. It would be a genuine spectator sport for him.

Wolff returned to the hill to start the next-to-last phase. The natives were just about finished loading the ship with black powder, ammonium nitrate, and mercury fulminate. The half-built craft consisted of two skeletons of hollow bamboo in which the gas cells had been installed. One was the lower decks of the planned ship; the upper part was supposed to be attached at a later date.

From the beginning, he had known that using the ship as a space traveler was impossible. He doubted very much that it would work, or, if it would, that the voyage between this world and Appirmatzum could be made. The odds were far too high against success.

But he had pretended confidence in it, and so the work had gone on. Moreover, any spy among the Lords, or any other monitor for Urizen, would have been fooled.

Perhaps Urizen was watching him now and wondering what he meant to do. If so, by the time he found out, it would be too late.

The natives released the two halves of the ship from its moorings. They rose several feet and then stopped, weighed down by the several tons of explosives. This altitude was all that Wolff desired. He gave the signal and the natives pushed the crafts up the hill until their prows were almost inside the frame. There was just enough room for the ship to slide through the frames. Wolff had ordered it built in two sections because the fully built ship could not have negotiated the space. Even the partial frames had only an inch on either side on top and bottom to spare.

Wolff lit the fuses on each side of the two floating frameworks and signaled his men. Chanting, they pushed the crafts on in. Wolff, standing to one side, could see the landscape of the island on the other side of the gate. The first ship seemed to be chewed up, or lopped off, as if floated through the gate-frame. Presently, all but the aft of the second was gone, and then that, too, had disappeared.

Luvah appeared from the jungle with Vala's unconscious body over his shoulder. Behind him were the other Lords, alarmed, puzzled, and angry or frightened. Wolff explained to them what he meant to do. He said, "I could tell no one except Luvah because I could trust no one else. I suspect Vala of spying for our father, but she may be innocent. However, I could not take a chance on her. So I had Luvah knock her out while she slept. We'll take her along in case she is not guilty. By the time she wakes up, she'll be in the midst of it. Too late for her to do anything then.

"Now, get into the suits. As I've explained, they'll operate under water as well as in space. Better, since they were designed for diving."

Luvah looked at the gate. "Do you think the explosives went off?"

Wolff shrugged and said, "There's no way of telling. It's a one-way gate, of course, so there'll be no indication from the other side. But I hope that by now Urizen's initial traps have been destroyed. And I hope he's very upset, wondering what we've done."

Luvah put a suit on Vala and then donned one himself. Wolff supervised the touching off of the fuses to the explosives planted at the bottom of the ditch around the hill. The fuses led through hollow bamboo pipes to the gunpowder, ammonium nitrate, and fulminate of mercury.

XV

THERE WAS a rumble and a shaking of the earth. Up rose the decayed vegetation and the roots in a great cloud of black smoke. When the debris had settled and the smoke had blown away, Wolff led the Lords towards the hill. It was sinking swiftly; its anchorage to the rest of the island severed and the lower part ripped apart. Under the weight of the heavy golden hexagons, it went down.

Wolff threw several fuse-lit bombs at the base of the gates to hasten the descent to the sea. The gates began to topple. Wolff held his men steady until the upper part struck the sides of the pit formed by the explosion. As the gates slid into the water below, he gave the order to jump. His mask over his face, the air tanks turned on, a flint-tipped spear in one hand, and a flint knife and flint axe in his belt, he leaped into the water.

The top of the gates disappeared just as he came up to the surface for a better look. The water was so foul with bits of roots and humus that he could not see anything. He grabbed the top of the frame and let its weight pull him down. It was on its way to the bottom of the sea, but he could go only a little way with it.

He felt Luvah, who was holding Vala in one arm, grab his ankle with the other. Another Lord should be getting hold of Luvah's ankle. Theotormon would be the only free swimmer until they got through the gate.

Wolff made sure, by feeling, that he was at the left gate. Then he began swimming. He had no trouble entering the gate. The inrush of sea-water carried him on in.

The current carried him down a long hall. The walls were self-luminous and radiated enough light for him to make out details. Some of the wall-plates were partially ripped off or bent. Down at the end of the hall, two thick white metal doors were twisted grotesquely. The explosion had done its work well. It was conceivable that the doors could have sealed off the rest of the palace from the flood of water. Eventually, the pressure of water from the sea bottom would have burst them open. By that time, the Lords would also have been dead from pressure.

Wolff went through the crumpled doors and on down another corridor. Seeing it come to an end, he twisted around until his feet were ahead of him. The water boiled at its end, striking the wall and then going off down a slightly sloping corridor. Wolff took the impact with his feet, shoved, and was off with the current down the hall. The light showed him a series of long metal spikes below him. Undoubtedly, they were prepared for the invading Lords, who were now passing above them.

The corridor suddenly dipped, and the water was racing down a fifty-degree angle. Wolff barely had time to see that it branched into two other corridors before he was carried helplessly out the great window at the end.

He fell, whirling over and over, seeing the palace walls rush by and a garden below. He was being hurled down by a cascade formed by the sea spouting out the window.

The crash into the pool at the bottom of the falls stunned him. Half-conscious, he swam up and away and was at the edge of the pool. Originally, the pool had been a sunken garden. Lucky for him, he thought, otherwise, he would have been smashed to death. He dragged himself up over the lip of stone, still clutching his spear.

The other Lords came bobbing up one by one. Theotormon was first. Luvah was next, with a conscious, and frightened, Vala behind him. Rintrah, swam in a few seconds later. Tharmas floated into the edge of the pool. He was face down, his arms, outspread. Wolff pulled him up and turned him over. He must have smashed into the side of the window before being carried out. His leg was snapped at the knee and the side of his face was crushed in.

Vala stormed at Wolff. He told her to shut up; they did not have time for talking. In a few words he explained what he had done and why.

Vala recovered quickly. She smiled, though still pale, and said, "You have done it again, Jadawin! Turned Urizen's own devices against him!"

"I do not know if you are guilty of allying yourself with our father or not," Wolff said. "Perhaps I am overly suspicious, though it may be impossible to be that when dealing with a Lord. If you are innocent, I will apologize. If not, well, our father must by now be convinced that you have betrayed him and are with us. So he will kill you before you can explain, unless you kill him first. You have no choice."

"Jadawin, you were always a fox! So be it! I will kill our father the first chance I get! Who knows, I may have the chance! I would have sworn up to a few hours ago that we would be trapped as soon as we entered his domain! But here we are, and he has a deadly problem on his hands!"

She pointed up at the great window through which the sea was cataracting. "Obviously the gate is on the highest level of the palace. And water flows downward. If he doesn't do something soon, he will be drowned like a rat caught in its own hole."

She turned to indicate the land outside the palace. "As you can see, the palace is in a valley surrounded entirely by high mountains. It will take some time, but the entire sea of the waterworld will come through the gates, unless the matching gates on the waterworld settle on a shallow bottom. This valley will be flooded, and then the water will spill over the mountains and inundate the rest of the planet.''

Rintrah said, ''Why don't we just climb the mountains and watch our father drown?''

Wolff shook his head. ''No, Chryseis is in there.''

Rintrah said, ''What is that to the rest of us?''

''Urizen will have flying craft,'' Wolff said. ''If he escapes the palace in one, he will pick us off. Even if we should hide from him, we would be doomed. He has merely to leave us here. Eventually, this world will be flooded. We will be trapped, perhaps to starve again. No, if you want to get away from here and back to your own universe, you will have to help me kill Urizen.''

He said to Theotormon, ''You were allowed a little freedom while you were his prisoner. If we could find the area you know, we could better avoid traps.''

''There is an entrance at the bottom of the sunken garden, which is now a pool,'' Theotormon said. ''That would be the best way to enter. We can swim up to the levels that are not yet flooded. If we avoid contact with the floor and walls, we can prevent setting off the traps.''

They plunged into the water and, hugging the sides of the pool to avoid the impact of the falling waters, swam around behind the cataract. It was easy to locate the door, since a current was roaring through it. They let it sweep them through until they came to a staircase. This was broad and built of sculptured red and black stone. They swam up it and after many turnings, came to another level. This, too, was flooded, so they continued their ascent. The next floor was inches deep in water and filling swiftly. The Lords climbed on up the stairs until they were on the fourth story.

Urizen's palace was like every Lord's, magnificent in every respect. At another time, Wolff might have lingered to look at the paintings, drapes, sculptures, and treasures, loot of many worlds. Now he had but two thoughts. Kill Urizen and save his great-eyed wife, Chryseis.

Wolff looked around before giving the word to advance. He said, "Where's Vala?"

"She was behind me a moment ago," Rintrah said.

"Then she's in no trouble," Wolff replied. "But *we* may be. If she's sneaked off to join Urizen . . ."

"We'd better get to him before she does," Luvah said.

Wolff led the way, expecting at every second a trap. There was, however, a chance that Urizen had not set any here. Undoubtedly, there would be defenses at every entrance. But Urizen may have thought himself safe here. Moreover, the water pouring through from above and below might have deactivated the power supplies. Whatever contingency Urizen had prepared himself for, he had never thought of another planet's seas emptying themselves into his domain.

Theotormon said, "The floor above is the one where I was kept prisoner. Urizen's private apartments are also there."

Wolff took the first staircase they came to. He walked up slowly, looking intently for signs of traps. They came without mishap to the next floor and then stood for a moment. The closer they got to Urizen, the more nervous they became. Their hate was beginning to be tinged with some of the old awe they had felt for him when they were children.

They were in a huge chamber, the walls of which were white marble. There were many bas-reliefs carved on them, scenes from many planets. One showed Urizen seated on a throne. Below him, a new universe was forming out of chaos. Another scene showed him standing in a meadow with children at play around him. Wolff recognized himself, his brothers, sisters, and cousins. Those had been happy times, even though there were shadows now and then to forecast the days of hate and anxiety.

Theotormon said, "You can hear the rumble of the water above. It won't be long until this floor, too, is flooded."

"Chryseis is probably held in the same area in which you were prisoner," Wolff said. "You lead the way there."

Theotormon, his rubbery legs acting as springs, went swiftly. He traced his way without hesitation through a series of rooms and halls that would have been a bewildering labyrinth to a stranger.

Theotormon stopped before a tall oval entrance of scarlet stone with purplish masses that formed ragged silhouettes of winged creatures. Beyond was a great chamber that glowed a dull red.

"That is the room in which I spent most of my time," he said. "But I fear to go through the doorway."

Wolff extended his spear through the archway. Theotormon said, "Wait a minute. It may have a delayed reaction to catch whoever goes on it."

Wolff continued to hold the spear. He counted the seconds, estimating how far within the chamber he would have gone if he walked on in. There was a flare of light that blinded him and sent him reeling back.

When he regained his sight, he saw that his spear was shorn off. Heat billowed out from the expanding air in the chamber, and there was the odor of charred wood.

"Lucky for you that most of the heat was localized and went upward," Theotormon said.

The trap covered about twenty yards. Beyond that the room might be safe. But how to get past the death that waited?

He stepped back some paces, cast the butt of the

spear through the archway, and turned his back. Again, light burst forth, driving the shadows of the Lords down along the corridor and then sending a wave of heat out after them. Wolff turned and threw an arrow into the room and gave the archway his back again while he counted. Three seconds passed before the trap was sprung again.

He gave an order and they returned to the level staircase, which was half below the rising waters. They put on their oxygen masks and dipped themselves into the water. Then they ran down the hall as swiftly as they could, hoping that the water would not dry off them. At the archway, Wolff tossed another arrow through. As soon as the light died, but before the heat had thoroughly dissipated, he dashed into the chamber. Behind him came Theotormon and Luvah. They had three seconds to cover twenty yards and a few feet. They made it. With the heat drying off the film of water on their suits and warming their backs. But they were through.

Rintrah cast an arrow into the room, and he and Tharmas ran into the heat. Wolff had turned around to watch them as soon as the light disappeared. He cried out because Tharmas had hesitated. Tharmas did not heed his warning to wait and try again, perhaps because he did not hear it. He was racing desperately, his eyes wide behind the goggles. Wolff shouted to the others to turn away as Rintrah sped past him. There was another nova of light, a scream, and a thud. Heat billowed over the Lords; they smelled the charred fish skin of the suit and burned human flesh.

Tharmas was a dark mass on the floor, his fingers and toes almost burned off.

Without a word, the others turned away and went on through the room. Near its other archway, Theotormon led them through a very narrow doorway, although he did not do so until after it had been tested. They came into a hemispherical room at least one hundred yards across. Within the room were many large cages, all empty except for one.

Wolff saw the occupant of the cage first.

He cried out, "Urizen!"

XVI

THE CAGE was ten feet by ten. It was furnished only with a thin blanket on the floor, a pipe for drinking water, a hole for excretion, and an automatic food dispenser. The man within it was very tall and very thin. He had the face of a bearded and starved falcon. His hair fell down his back to his calves, and his beard hung below his knees. The black hairs were threaded with gray, by which Wolff knew that his father had been a long time in the cage. Even after the so-called immortality drugs were cut off, their effect lasted for years.

Urizen advanced towards the bars but he was careful not to touch them. Wolff warned the others back in a low voice. He walked up to the bars as if he meant to grip them. Urizen watched him with deep-sunken and feverish eyes but did not open his mouth. A few inches from the bars, Wolff stopped and said, "Do you still hate us so much, Father, that you would let us die?"

He raked the bars with the tip of an arrow; veins of light ran over the metal.

Urizen smiled grimly and spoke in a hollow, pain-shot voice, "Touching the bars is only painful, not fatal. Ah, Jadawin, you were always a fox! No one but you could have gotten this far. No one but you and your sister, Vala, and perhaps Red Orc."

"So she did evade all your traps and snared the snarer," Wolff said. "She is indeed a remarkable woman, my sister."

"Where is she?" Urizen asked. "Did she die this time? I know that she was with you because she told me what she intended to do."

"She is in the palace and still to be reckoned

with," Wolff said. "All this time, she had us convinced that you were in the Seat of Power. She was playing with us, sharing our dangers, pretending to be our ally. I suspected her of working with you, but this . . . I never dreamed of."

"I am doomed," Urizen said. "I cannot get out; you cannot open this cage to release me. Even if you wanted to, you could not. And I must die soon unless I can get help. Vala has implanted a slowly acting and painful cancerous growth within me. In fact, she has done this three times, only to remove it each time before I died and then nurse me back to health."

"I would be lying if I said I was sorry, and you know it," Wolff said. "You are getting what you deserve."

"Moral lectures from you, Jadawin!" Urizen said. His eyes blazed with the old fire, and Wolff felt something within him quail. The dread of his father had not died yet.

"I heard that you had changed much since your life on Earth, but I could not believe it. Now I know it is true."

"I did not come here to argue with you," Wolff said. "There is little time for talk left, anyway. Tell me, Father, how we can get to the control room safely. If you want vengeance, you must tell us. Vala is loose again and probably in the control room right now."

Urizen said, "Why should I tell you anything? I am going to die, but I will at least have the pleasure of knowing that you, Rintrah, Luvah, and Theotormon will die with me."

"Does it give you pleasure to know that Vala will triumph? That she will live on? That your body, too, will be stuffed and mounted in the trophy hall?"

Urizen smiled bitterly. "If I tell you what you want, then Vala might die, but you would live. It is a loathsome choice to make. Either way, I lose."

"You may hate us," Wolff said, "but we have never done anything to you. Yet Vala . . ."

Theotormon said, "The seas will soon be flooding this level. Then we all die. And Vala, safe in her control room, will laugh. And she will take whatever vengeance she has been planning against Chryseis."

Wolff felt helpless. He could not threaten Urizen to make him talk. What more could he do to him than had been done?

He said, "Let's go. We can't waste any more time." To Urizen, he said, "Good-bye forever, Father. You must die and soon. You hold revenge against Vala in your heart, and if you would unlock your lips, you would get it. But hatred blinds you and makes you rob yourself."

Urizen called after them, "Wait!"

Eagerly, Wolff returned to the cage. Urizen licked his lips and said, "If I tell you, will you do me one favor?"

"I can't free you, Father," Wolff said. "You know we have no time to figure out how to do it. Moreover, even if I could, I wouldn't. I would kill you before I would loose you upon the world."

"The favor I trade is exactly that," Urizen said. "Death. I am suffering agonies, my son. My pride forbade me to say so until now. But one more minute of this life seems like a thousand years to me. If it were not for my pride, I would have gone down on my knees before you long ago, would have begged you to put me out of my torture. That I would never do. Urizen does not beg. But a trade, that is another thing."

"I agree," Wolff said. "An arrow between the bars will do it."

Urizen whispered and in a few words told them what they needed to know. He had just finished when there was laughter at the far end of the room. Wolff whirled to see Vala walking towards them. He fitted an arrow to a bow-string, knowing as he did so that Vala would not have shown herself unless she felt sufficiently protected.

Then he saw through Vala to the wall behind her and knew that it was a projection. He hoped that she had not also overheard Urizen. If she had, she would be able to do what she wished with them.

"I could not have done better if I had planned it this way," her image said. "It is fitting, and my greatest desire, to have all of you die together. A happy family reunion! You may witness each other's death struggles. How nice!

"And I will be leaving this planet and this universe and may then trap the surviving brother, and my beloved sister, Anana. Only I will rest for a while and amuse myself with your Chryseis."

"You have failed so far, and you will continue to fail!" Wolff shouted. "Even if you kill us, you will not live long to enjoy your triumph! You know about the *etsfagwo* poison of the natives of the waterworld, don't you? How it can be served in food and leaves no taste? How it goes through the veins and stays there for a long time with no ill effect? And then it suddenly reacts and doubles the victim up in terrible pain that lasts for hours? And how there is no antidote?

"Well, Vala, I suspected you of treachery. So I had the *etsfagwo* put in your supper last night. It will soon take hold of you, Vala, and then you will not be able to laugh about us."

Wolff had not done this and until this moment had not even thought of doing so. But he was determined that if he died, Vala would pay for it with some hours of mental anguish.

The image screamed with fury and desperation. It

said, "You are lying, Jadawin! You would not do this; you could not! You are just trying to scare me!"

"You will know whether I tell the truth or not in a very short time!" Wolff shouted. He turned to shoot the arrow through the bars of the cage to fulfill his promise to Urizen. As he shifted, he saw Vala's image flicker out of existence. Immediately thereafter, a green foam spurted out of hidden pipes in the ceiling. It shot down with great force, spread out, rose to the knees of the Lords, and set them to coughing with its acrid fumes. Wolff's eyes watered, and he bent over. He leaned down to pick up the bow and arrow which he had dropped. The fumes made him cough even more violently.

Suddenly, the foam was to his neck. He struggled to get through it and to the door at the far end, although there might be another trap waiting there. The foam rose above his head. He held his breath while he put his air-mask on. Then he lifted it a little from his face and blew out the foam it had collected. He hoped the others had enough presence of mind to think of their masks.

Within a few steps of the exit, he felt the foam begin to harden. He strove against it, pushing as hard as he could. It continued to resist him, to reduce his progress to a very slow motion. Abruptly, the foam became a jelly and the green opacity cleared away. He was caught like a fly in amber.

Wolff could not see the others, who were behind him. He was facing the archway towards which he had struggled. He tried to move his arms and legs and found that he could make a little progress. With a vast effort, he could shove himself forward less than an inch. Then the jelly, like a tide, moved him back again and settled around him. There was nothing he could do except wait for his air supply to run out. The breathing system was a closed system, one that re-used air and did not dissipate the carbon dioxide. If it had been an open system, he would have been dead already. The jelly closed in around so tightly that there would have been no place for the breathed-out carbon dioxide to go.

He had perhaps a half-hour of life remaining. Vala would be laughing now. And Chryseis, great-eyed beautiful Chryseis, what was she doing? Was she being forced to watch this scene? Or was she listening to Vala's descriptions of what Vala intended for her?

Fifteen minutes passed by with his every thought seeking a way out. There was none. This was the end of over 25,000 years of life and the powers of a god. He had lived for nothing; he might as well never have been born. He would die, and Chryseis would die, and both would be stuffed and mounted and placed on exhibit in the trophy hall.

No, that was not true, at least. Vala would have to abandon this place. The waters roaring through the permanent gate at the top level of the palace would ensure that. She would be denied this pleasure. His body, and Chryseis', would lie beneath a sea, in darkness and cold, until the flesh rotted and the bones were tossed back and forth by the currents and strewn about.

The waters! He had forgotten that they were racing through the halls of the levels above and down the staircases. If only . . .

The first rush half-filled the corridor beyond the archway and ripped out a chunk of jelly. The corridor was quickly filled, and the jelly began to dissolve. The process took time, however. The waters crept towards him, eating their way and turning the jelly into a green foam that was absorbed by the liquid. More than half an hour had passed since he had estimated that he had about thirty minutes of air left.

He felt that every breath would be his last.

The jelly became green foam and obscured his vision. The thick stuff melted away, and he was free. But now he was in as much danger as before. Submerged in water, he would drown as soon as the air ran out.

He swam towards the others, whom he could see through a green veil. He yanked them loose from the jelly that still held them, only to find that Rintrah was dead. He had gotten his mask on in time but something had gone wrong. Wolff gestured at Theotormon and Luvah and swam towards the other exit. It opened to their only hope. To try to go through the door through which the seas were pushing was impossible because of the current. They were carried, like it or not, towards the other archway.

Wolff dug at the jelly which clogged the doorway until it broke loose, and he was carried headlong into the next room. His brothers came at his heels and slid on their faces across the room and piled into him against the opposite wall. They rolled out of the stream and were on their feet. Wolff turned the air off and lifted his mask. He not only had to speak to them, but there would be a minute or two before the room filled in which they could conserve what little supply remained in the tanks.

"Urizen told me that there is a secret door to a duplicate control room! He had it prepared in case somebody ever did get into the main control room! It has controls which will deactivate those of the main room! But to get to it, we have to go through the doorway with the heat-ray trap. He didn't have time to tell me how to turn off the heat-rays! We'll put our masks back on when the water gets too high and then go through. The water should knock the projectors out! I hope!"

They placed the masks over their faces and

crouched in a corner near the archway to gain protection from the full force of the current. The sea struck the wall opposite the archway and then raced off down the floor and through the door. Seeing that the water was not activating the rays, Wolff hurled his stone axe towards the door. Even through his closed lids, he saw the dazzle. When he opened his eyes, the water was boiling. The axe had been swept on through the arch.

The waters rose swiftly, carrying the treading Lords up towards the ceiling. When there was only a foot of air between the sea and the ceiling, they put on their masks. Wolff dived as close towards the floor as he could get and began swimming. Suddenly, the air shut off. He held his breath and continued swimming. There was a glare of light that blinded him, and the water seemed to burn his exposed hands and back of neck. He bumped against the side of the arch and was borne out into the next room. Here he shoved his feet against the floor and propelled himself upward. He held his hands out to soften the impact against the ceiling, which he could not yet see.

His head bumping against stone, he removed his mask and breathed in. His lungs filled with air, then water slapped him in the mouth and he coughed. His vision returned; Theotormon and Luvah were beside him. Wolff lifted his hand and pointed downward. "Follow me!"

He dived, his eyes open, his hands sliding along the wall. There was a green jade statue, a foot high, once an idol of some people in some universe, squatting in a niche. Wolff rotated its head, and a section of the wall opened inwards. The three Lords were carried into the large room. They scrambled to their feet, and Wolff ran to a console and pulled on a red-handled lever. The door closed slowly against the pressure of the water, leaving a foot of water in the room.

Identifying the console Urizen had told him about (there were at least thirty), Wolff pressed down a rectangular plate on which was an ideogram of the ancient writing once used by the Lords. He stepped back with the first smile he had had for a long time.

"Vala not only won't be able to use her controls any more," he said, "she's trapped in her control room as well. And all gates of escape in the room are deactivated. Only the permanent gates in the palace, like the gate to the waterworld, are still on."

Wolff reached towards the button that would activate the viewscreen in the other control room. He withdrew his hand and stood in thought for a moment.

"The less our sister knows of the true situation, the better for us," he said. "Theotormon, come here and listen carefully."

Wolff and Luvah hid behind a console and peered through a narrow opening between the console and its screen. Theotormon pushed the button with the end of his flipper. Vala was staring at him, her long hair dark-red with damp and her face twisted with fury.

"You!" she said.

"Greetings, sister," Theotormon answered. "Are you surprised to see me still living? And how do you feel knowing that I have sealed off your escape and rendered you powerless?"

"Where are your brothers, your betters?" Vala said, trying to see past him into the room.

"They're dead. Their airtanks gave out and so did mine. But this body that our father gave me enabled me to hold my breath until the water washed away your jelly."

"So Jadawin is finally dead? I don't believe it. You

are trying to play a trick on me, you stupid slug!"

"You're in no position to call names."

"Let me see his body," she said.

Theotormon shrugged. "That's impossible. He's floating somewhere in the palace. I barely made it to this room myself. I can't go out to get him without flooding this room."

Vala looked at the water on the floor and then she smiled. "So you're trapped, too. You fish-stinking idiot, you don't even have the brains of a fish! You just told me what your situation is!"

Theotormon gaped. He said, "But . . . but . . ."

"You may think you have me in your power," Vala said. "And so you do, in a manner of speaking. But you are just as much in mine. I know where the spacecraft is. It can get us off this planet and to another, which has a gate through which we can leave this universe. Now, what do you propose to do about this impasse?"

Theotormon scratched the fur on his head with the tip of a flipper. "I don't know."

"Oh, yes, you do! You're stupid, but not that stupid! You'll make a trade with me. You let me out, and I'll let you leave with me in the ship. There's no other way out for either of us."

Wolff could not see Theotormon's expression, but he could deduce from his tone the cunningness and suspicion on his face.

"How do I know I can trust you?"

"You don't, any more than I can trust you. We'll have to arrange this so neither of us can possibly trip the other up. Do you agree?"

"Well, I don't know . . ."

"This control room won't be harmed if the seas get a mile high and sit forever on the palace. I have food and water enough for a year. I can just sit here and let you die. And then I'll figure some way to get out, believe me. I'll discover a way.''

''In that case,'' Theotormon said, ''why don't you do it?''

''Because I don't want to stay in this room for a year. I have too many things to do.''

''All right. But what about Chryseis?''

''She comes with me. I have plans for her,'' Vala said.

Her voice became even more suspicious. ''Why should you care about her?''

''I don't. I just wondered. Maybe . . . maybe you could give her to me. From what Jadawin said, she must be very beautiful.''

Vala laughed and said, ''That would be one form of torture for her. But it isn't enough. No, you can't have her.''

''Then it's not a deal,'' Theotormon said. ''You keep her. See how you like being cooped up with her for a year. Besides, I don't really think you can swim to the spacecraft. The water pressure will be too much.''

Vala said, ''You stupid selfish slimegut! You'd die yourself rather than let me have anything! Very well, take her then!''

Wolff smiled. He had told Theotormon to bring up Chryseis and so take her mind off him. This business about Chryseis was just irrelevant enough and so Theotormonically selfish that she might be convinced that he was not hiding the truth.

Theotormon clapped his flippers together with glee. Wolff hoped that his joy was all act, since he was not sure that Theotormon might not betray him at the last moment. Theotormon said, ''All right. Now, how can we get to the spacecraft?''

''You'll have to release me first. I'm not going to

tell you and then have you take off without me."

"But if I open the door to your room, you'll be able to get out ahead of me."

"Can't you set the controls so they'll open the doors by the time you get here?"

Theotormon grunted as if the thought were a new one. "All right. Only, you'll have to come out of the room with absolutely no clothes on. You must both be nude and emptyhanded. I'll come out of my room weaponless. We'll both leave at exactly the same time and meet in the corridor that links the two rooms."

Vala gasped and said, "I thought . . . ! You mean you knew all the time how to get here . . . so that's where the other controls are! And I thought the other end of the corridor was a wall."

"It won't do you any good to know," Theotormon said. "You can't get out until I let you. Oh, yes, strip Chryseis, too. I don't want you to hide any weapons on her."

Vala said, "You're not taking any chances, are you? Perhaps you're more intelligent than I thought."

What was she planning? If she did meet him in the middle of the corridor, she would be helpless against Theotormon's far greater strength. He would attack her the moment she revealed the location of the spacecraft, and she must know that.

The truth was that Wolff, Luvah, and Theotormon knew where the ship was. Theotormon had pretended ignorance only to seem to give her an advantage. She had to be lured out of the room, otherwise she would never come out. Wolff knew his sister. She would die and take Chryseis with her rather than surrender. To her it was inconceivable that a Lord would keep a promise not to harm her. She had good reason. In fact, Wolff himself, though he never thought of himself as a genuine Lord anymore, was not sure he would have kept his word to her. Certainly, he did not intend that Theotormon adhere to his assurances.

Then what did she have in mind?

Theotormon went over the method of conduct with Vala again, pretending that he was not quite sure. Then he deactivated the screen and turned to Wolff and Luvah. Wolff opened the door into the corridor so that he and Luvah could go out ahead of time. As Theotormon had said, the corridor linked the two control rooms. Both control rooms and the hall between were in an enclosed unit of fourteen feet-thick metal alloy. The unit could hold any pressure of water and was resistant even to a direct hit by a hydrogen bomb. The interior wall was coated with a substance which would repel the neutrons of a neutron bomb. Urizen had placed the secret control room in this unit, near the main control room for just such situations as this. Anyone who managed to get into the main room would not know that there was an exit to the corridor until part of the seemingly solid wall of the main control room opened.

The corridor itself, though an emergency convenience, had been furnished as if a reception for Lords were to be held in it. It contained paintings, sculptures, and furniture that a Terrestrial billionaire could not have purchased with all his fortune. A chandelier made from a single carved diamond, weighing half a ton, hung from a huge gold alloy chain. And this was not the most valuable object in the corridor.

Wolff hid behind a davenport covered with the silky chocolate-and-azure hide of an animal. Luvah concealed himself behind the base of a statue. Theotormon made sure that they were ready and returned to the control room to inform Vala that they could now proceed to meet each other as planned.

He then pressed the button that operated the door to Vala's room.

The wall at the other end of the corridor slid upwards. Light poured out of the opening, and Vala stuck her head cautiously around the frame. Theotormon did the same from his door. He stepped out quickly, ready to hurl himself back if she had a weapon. She gave a low laugh and came out of the doorway, her hands held out to show their emptiness. She was naked and magnificent.

Wolff gave her a glance. He had eyes only for the woman who followed her. It was his Chryseis, the beautiful huge-eyed nymph with tiger-striped hair. She, too, was unclothed.

"The Horn of Shambarimen," Theotormon said. "I almost forgot! Where is it?"

"It is in the control room," Vala replied. "I did not bring it because you told me to be empty-handed."

"Go get it, Chryseis," Theotormon said. "But when you return with it, hold it up above your head at arm's length and do not point it at me. If you make a sudden motion with it, I will kill you."

Vala's laughter filled the corridor. "Are you so suspicious that you suspect even her? She would not hurt you! She is definitely not going to do anything for me!"

Theotormon did not reply. Instructed by Wolff, he was playing the role of the overly alert Lord to keep Vala from suspecting any treachery. If Theotormon had been too trusting, she would have scented something foul at once.

Vala and Theotormon then advanced towards each other, taking a step forward slowly and in unison. It was as if they were partners in a formal dance, they moved so stately and in such matching rhythm.

Wolff crouched and waited. He had taken his suit off so that it would not hinder his movements. The sweat of tension covered his body. Neither he nor Luvah were armed. They had lost all their own weapons before they reached the secret room. And the room, to his dismay, had contained no arms. Apparently, Urizen had not thought it necessary. Or, much more likely, there were weapons hidden behind the walls, accessible only to one who knew how to find them. Urizen had not had time to give that information—if he had ever intended to do so.

The plan was to wait until Vala had passed Luvah, hidden on the other side of the hall. When he rushed out behind her, Theotormon would jump her. Wolff would hurl himself from his hiding palace and help the other two.

Vala stopped several feet away from the diamond chandelier. Theotormon also stopped. She said, "Well, my ugly brother, it seems that you have kept your side of the bargain."

He nodded and said, "So where is the spaceship?"

He went forward one step in the hope that she, too, would take one and so place herself nearer. Vala stood still, however. Mockingly, she said, "The entrance to it is just on the other side of that rose-shaped mirror. You could have gone to it and left me to die—if you had known about it! You witless filth!"

Theotormon snarled and leaped at her. Luvah came out from behind the statue but bumped into Chryseis. Wolff rose and sped straight at Vala.

She screamed and held up her right hand, the palm at right angles to her arm, fingers stiffly pointing toward the ceiling. Out of the palm shot an intensely white beam no thicker than a needle. She moved her hand to her left in a horizontal arc. The beam slashed across Theotormon's neck, and his head fell off. For a moment, the body stood upright, blood fountaining upward from his neck. Then he fell forward.

Wolff whirled like a broken-field runner. He threw

himself down on the floor behind Theotormon's feet. Vala, hearing Luvah curse as he recovered from his bump into Chryseis, spun around. Evidently she thought that this was the nearest danger and that she had enough time to deal with Wolff.

Chryseis had reacted quickly. On seeing the head of the seal-man fall off and roll back behind Theotormon, she had dived for the protection of a statue. Vala's ray took off a chunk of the base of the statue but missed Chryseis. Then Luvah was coming in, head down. Vala leaped adroitly aside and chopped down with the edge of the palm of her left hand. Luvah fell forward on his face, unconscious.

Why she had not killed him with the tiny beamer implanted in the flesh of her palm was a mystery. Perhaps she wanted someone to save as a torture victim, in keeping with the psychology of the Lords.

Wolff was helpless, or so Vala thought. She advanced towards him.

"You I shall kill now," she said. "You're too dangerous to leave alive for a second longer than necessary."

"I'm not dead yet," Wolff said. His fingers closed on Theotormon's head, and he hurled it at her. He was up on his feet at once and running towards her, knowing that he did not have a chance but hoping that something would happen to deflect her aim long enough.

She raised her hand to ward off the grisly projectile. The beam split the head in half, but one section continued to fly towards her.

The ray, directed towards the ceiling momentarily, cut the gold alloy chain. And the half-ton diamond chandelier came down upon her.

Wolff was still charging while all this occurred. He dived on the floor to be below her line of fire in case she was still living and could use the hand. She glared up at him, the light not yet gone from her eyes. Her arms and her body were pinned beneath the diamond, from beneath which blood ran.

"You . . . did it, brother," she gasped.

Chryseis came out from behind the statue to throw herself in his arms. She clung to him and sobbed. He could not blame her for this, but there were still things to do.

He kissed her a few times, hugged her, and pushed her away from him.

"We have to get out while we can," he said. "Push in on the third gargoyle to the left on the upper decoration on that mirror."

She did so; the mirror swung in. Wolff put his unconscious brother on his shoulders and started towards the entrance. Chyrseis said, "Robert! What about her?"

He stopped. "What about her?"

"Are you going to let her suffer like this? It may take a long time before she dies."

"I don't think so," he said. "Besides, she has it coming."

"Robert!"

Wolff sighed. For a moment, he had been a complete Lord again, had become the old Jadawin.

He put Luvah on the floor and walked over to Vala. She twisted, and her hand came loose, a section of the shorn diamond falling over onto the floor. Wolff leaped at her and caught her hand just as the ray shot forth from the palm. He twisted her hand so violently that the bones cracked. She cried out once with pain before she died.

Directed by Wolff, the laser beam had half-guillotined her.

Wolff, Chryseis, and Luvah entered the spaceship. It rose straight up the launching shaft to the very top of the palace. Wolff headed the ship for the exit-gate, hidden in the mountains of the tempusfudger planet. Only then did he have time to find out how Vala had managed to get Chryseis from her bed and out of their world.

"The hexaculum awoke me," she said, "while you were still sleeping. It—Vala's voice—warned me that if I tried to wake you, you would be killed in a horrible way. Vala told me that only by following her instructions would I prevent your death."

"You should have known better," he said. "If she had been able to hurt me, she would have done it. But then, I suppose that you were too concerned for me. You did not dare to take the chance that she might be bluffing."

"Yes. I wanted to cry out, but I was afraid that she might be able to carry out her threats. I was so terrified for you that I was not thinking straight. So I went through the gate she designated, one of those gates that take you to a lower level of our planet. I deactivated the alarms before entering it, as she ordered. Vala was waiting in the cave where our gate took me. She had already set up a gate to take us to this universe. The rest you know."

Wolff turned the controls over to Luvah so that he could embrace and kiss her. She began to weep, and soon he was weeping, too. His tears were not only from relief for having gotten her back unharmed and relief from the unrelenting strain of the experiences in this world. He wept for his dead brothers and sister. He did not mourn those who had just died, the adults. He mourned for his brothers and sister as the children they had once been and for the love they had had for each other as children. He grieved for the loss of what they might have been.